The Mysterious Phone Call

A Mud Street Misfits Adventure
Book 2

By
Brian O'Dell
and
Beth Lauderdale

MUD STREET
GIG H

O'Dell & Lauderdale/Mud Street Misfits LLC
11010 Harbor Hill Drive NW #B616
Gig Harbor, Washington 98332

www.mudstreetmisfits.com

Publisher's Note: This is a work of fiction. Names, characters, places, and incidents are a product of the authors' imagination. Locales and public names are sometimes used for atmospheric purposes. Any resemblance to actual people, living or dead, or to businesses, companies, events, institutions, or locales is completely coincidental.

Book cover design © 2019 Mud Street Misfits LLC

Ordering Information: Special discounts are available on quantity purchases by corporations, associations, and others. For details, contact the publisher at the address above.

Gig Harbor / O'Dell & Lauderdale — First Edition

ISBN 978-1-7326723-2-1

Printed in the United States of America

For my little Misfits;
Liam, Molly, Colin, and Emmett
~ BO

For my Misfit sis, Terre, who is always an
inspiration.
~ BL

PROLOGUE

S arah studied the old building through the rapidly descending dusk. Unlike the front, with its massive marquis and glass-fronted façade, the back was two stories of nondescript dirty-red brick. The door in front of her, which she already knew was securely locked, had probably once been the entrance for actors and musicians booked to perform on the ancient stage.

The Orpheum sat on the town square, flanked by other buildings—some older, some newer—and had been closed and abandoned for decades. To Sarah, it loomed larger-than-life and enthralled her like a mesmerist with his subject. *What is it about this place that intrigues me?* She had no idea. But ever since she'd laid eyes on the theater, she'd wanted to get inside. When Liam came up with the plan to sneak in and spend the night, she'd been nervous but excited, too. This would be her chance to finally see what lay beyond the disheveled exterior.

"Look up," Connor hissed in her ear.

Above her head, through the branches of the giant oak that shaded the back lot, Sarah could barely make out a fire escape ladder dangling among the leaves.

"Awesome," she whispered. "There's gotta be a door or window up there. Maybe one of them is unlocked?"

Liam was the tallest, but no matter how high he stretched, he couldn't reach the lower rung. He tried jumping but still couldn't grab it. "We need a ladder or I can try climbing the tree."

"Nah, the branches are too thin on that side," Connor said. "I've got an idea. Liam,

He helped Sarah to her feet and she led the way up the ladder. When they were all perched on the iron-grated landing, Liam tried the doorknob, but it wouldn't budge. He shoved at the door with his shoulder and then Connor joined him.

Nothing!

Liam stepped to the window and reached for the sill. He looked back at the group. "Fingers crossed, 'cause if this doesn't work, I'm out of ideas." He grasped the base of the window and heaved.

Nothing!

"Connor, help him," Sarah admonished.

When, together they still couldn't open the window, frustration gnawed at her. They had to help Liam and spending the night in the Orpheum was the first step in the only plan they had. They were quickly running out of options.

"The little twerps came around here, I'm sure of it." An all-too-familiar voice floated up from below. "And I heard some kind of metallic sound."

Sarah whirled and looked over the railing. Brandon, Kaylee, and Dylan stood right beneath them.

"Oh no," Molly whispered. "What do we do now?"

If those kids saw them, they were dead. Still as stones, the Misfits watched as the three bullies scanned the back of the building and kicked at the bushes where their bikes were hidden. *Don't look up, don't look up.* Sarah chanted silently, mentally pushing the kids away.

Minutes ticked by, and when Brandon and his crew finally disappeared around the corner of the building, Sarah sagged against the rail. They'd survived, for now at least, but they still needed to get into the Orpheum.

She heard a quiet tapping and turned back to the building. The noise seemed to be coming from the other side of the door. The tapping turned to rattling, then a deep groaning sound as metal rubbed against metal. As impossible as it seemed, the door was shaking in its frame. Then, with a shower of dust and paint chips, it popped open.

"What the heck?" Connor gaped.

"It was painted shut. You can see the dried globs," Sarah said, examining the jamb.

"Yeah, but what opened it?" Molly asked.

Connor shrugged. "We must have set off some kind of chain reaction."

"Just another bizarre thing in a long list of weird," Liam said. "But at least we're in." He stepped into the dark room, stomped a few paces away and then came back. "The floor seems solid. Come on in."

Sarah stared at the blackness yawning on the other side of the open door. The Orpheum! This was her chance to finally see what lay inside and yet ... The waiting darkness seemed like an abyss, impossible to climb out of. *Sarah, Sarah,* the building seemed to whisper to her. A part of her wanted to resist, but curiosity was stronger.

She took a deep breath and sidled in after her friends and brother. With a final glance outside, she pulled the door shut behind them.

CHAPTER ONE

Sarah slid pink cat-eye glasses onto her face and stared at herself in the antique mirror. It was early morning, and the pale gray of a sleepless night dusted below her brown eyes. No matter what combinations she tried, her multicolored outfit with its mismatched socks seemed dull. The news from her moms had been a shock, and the questions she hadn't asked had rumbled around in her head all night. There were tons of them, but the biggest one was; *Why do we have to leave? My whole life is here. And what about the Misfits?*

Sarah had been included in a sort of *club* with her best friends Liam and Connor. Liam was an amazing musician and had just gotten back from playing at Carnegie Hall with other kids who'd been recognized for their musical achievements. Connor was ... well, Connor. The way he saw the world sometimes made her laugh until her cheeks hurt and sometimes drove her insane. Her younger brother, David, and Liam's sister, Molly, were part of the club, too. They called themselves the Mud Street Misfits because they all lived on Mud Street and, not too long ago, they'd saved a man's life. How could she leave all that behind?

She sighed and reached back into the closet for her favorite purple hat. *Maybe this will make me feel better*, she thought, and clamped it down over her chestnut curls.

David was already eating cereal at the kitchen table and that never happened. He was dressed in his usual jeans and black tee shirt but his hair spiked out in a free-for-all that told Sarah he hadn't bothered to look in the mirror. She nudged him on the shoulder as she walked by, and he grunted a good morning.

"You didn't sleep much either, did you?" she said.

"No."

"It really sucks. The move, I mean." Sarah sighed.

She started to dig a frozen waffle out of the box, but the thought of food made her stomach clench. Maybe she'd feel like eating again someday, but not now.

"I know," David said, waving his spoon to emphasize the injustice of what their moms were doing. "I just don't understand. Why can't Mom-Rachel just find a better job here? Why do we have to go all the way to Chicago?"

Sarah just shook her head. "I'm leaving for school early so I can stop by the museum."

"Are you going to talk to Mom about the move?"

"Yeah. Maybe I can change her mind and get her to convince Rachel. Wish me luck."

***

The Ozark Historical Museum was in a small red-brick house two blocks off the square. In the early 1800s, it'd been the home for one of the town's founding fathers. Sarah thought the ornate Victorian architecture was beautiful, even if it was a bit fussy. Her mom had worked hard to get it and four other buildings into the historical registry so they could be preserved. Each one had been special, and Sarah was proud of her mom for fighting to protect them.

Sarah locked her bike into the rack and hurried up the steps to the wooden porch. She started to rap the brass knocker, then realized that the door was ajar. A tickle of concern shivered down the back of her neck. Her mom always kept the door locked unless it was during business hours. Carefully, she stepped into the warmth of the foyer. Raised voices echoed from the display area that had once been the living room.

"We can't go around saving every building in this town just because it's old," the mayor snarled. "Growth and progress. That is what this town needs, not wallowing in the past."

Quickly, Sarah ducked back. Then, cautiously, peeked around the corner.

Mayor Scott was a short, rotund man who always wore suits that looked just a little bit too small for him. Sarah wasn't sure how he'd gotten elected mayor, because he didn't really seem to like anyone.

"I understand that we need new buildings," Sarah's mom said. "I want the town to grow as well. But there are plenty of spots in this area to put up condos. We don't need to tear down a historic theater to do it."

Sarah clapped her hand over her mouth to hold back a gasp. They were talking about the Orpheum. In her dismay over moving, she'd forgotten about the demolition notice posted at the front entrance to the theater.

"That eyesore is sitting on prime real estate, right on the square."

The mayor took a step closer to her mom, and Sarah immediately stepped out of hiding.

When he spotted her, the thunderstorm of his face darkened.

He turned back to her mother, leaning in as if to make a point. "Just being old does not make a building important." He grabbed some papers off the counter and tried to arrange them into a tidy pile, but his hands were shaking too much. With a muffled curse, he wadded the papers into a ball and shoved them into his pocket. "That structure is not designated as a historical site. We will be tearing it down. Good day!"

The mayor walked quickly toward the door, scowling at Sarah as he passed. She and her mother both jumped when the door slammed shut behind him.

"Wow." Sarah pulled off her coat. "He was really mad."

"Yes! He came in to pick up some paperwork on the Orpheum, and I made the mistake of pointing out the importance of maintaining our historic buildings. He didn't like the idea that the city's historical society might oppose him."

"Mom, you have to do something! The Orpheum's been here since the Civil War. It has to have an amazing history that's important to this town."

"I know, but there's no proof that it has historical significance." Heather sighed. "Without that, it's just an old building, and he's going to tear it down."

"He can't do that."

"Sadly, honey, he can. The city owns the building now, and he can do whatever he wants with it. The mayor and his cronies want condos, so that's what they'll get."

"Can't you get it certified, you know, like the others?"

Heather sighed and sat in her office chair. It creaked as she rocked gently. "I don't know if I could or not but it doesn't matter, because we'll be gone."

Sarah took a deep breath. *Now is the best time. If I can explain to her how much David and I want to stay, then ... maybe.*

"Mom, why do we have to leave? I thought you liked it here."

"I do, very much, but this is a chance for Rachel to get that partnership she's always wanted."

"Can't she do that with Hoskins, Bradley, and Wayne? She's worked there for years."

"Apparently not. I'm sorry, Sarah. There's no other choice. The Chicago offer is too good to pass up."

"But Mom... David and I want to stay. We have our friends, school."

"I know, sweetie. I don't really want to start over again either." She put her arms around Sarah and laid her cheek on her hair. "You know how much we love you, right? This will be a good thing for all of us." With a sigh and a quick squeeze, she stepped back. "You and David have always adapted well to new places. You'll be fine this time, too."

As a doughy ball of sadness formed in her throat, Sarah knew she'd lost. A tear slipped down her cheek, and she quickly dashed it away. For her entire life, she'd never been able to say the right words when she needed to and this time was no different. *I was crazy to think I could ever convince the moms to change their minds. Poor David*, she thought. *Heck, poor me. Another town, another school, another set of strange faces.*

***

Sarah pushed her bike across the commons toward the park. *It isn't fair. Why does a job matter so much? Family, friends, home ... roots, that's what's important.* She was deep into a mental tirade when a voice dragged her out.

"Sarah? Is that you?"

She glanced up to see a man, gray hair sticking out from under a faded ball cap, sitting on one of the park benches. At first, she wasn't sure who he was, and then she recognized him. "Mr. Ortman, hi." She steered her bike over. "What're you doing here?"

"Oh, just sitting and thinking about my Elaine. I told you about her when you kids brought back my record album. Today's our anniversary, and I miss her like crazy. Times like this, I like to come back to Ozark and remember the life we had here. Now, don't get me wrong. I'm grateful that Greg moved me in with him, but Kenosha just doesn't feel like home. I don't know if it ever will."

"Yeah, I know what you mean," Sarah said, sitting down next to him. "Home seems to be a hard place to find."

"So, how're your friends doing?" Mr. Ortman asked. "That Liam sure has an amazing gift."

Sarah's eyes widened and she looked at the man sharply. *Does he know about Liam's psychic ability? How could he? We all swore not to tell.*

"Uh ... er. His gift?"

"That's what I'd call it. Greg and I heard him play that bass of his with a jazz group a few nights ago." Mr. Ortman shook his head. "Pretty darn amazing."

"Oh, that." Sarah almost laughed. "Yeah, he's pretty good."

"More than good, Sarah. Much more than good."

She gestured toward the old theater. "Did you hear they're going to tear it down?"

"The Orpheum? Now, that's a damn shame. Pardon my French, but that building is beautiful."

"Mayor Scott wants to build condos on the land."

"Harrumph," the old man snorted. "That sounds typical of the politicians these days. Tear down beauty and throw up the cheap. You ever hear the old Joanie Mitchell song, 'Big Yellow Taxi'?"

Sarah shook her head.

"It's about appreciating what you've got and that progress for the sake of progress isn't always the best thing." He sang the chorus softy.

"That is really the truth. It's history and the people who lived it that's important. Things should be preserved so that us kids can enjoy them, too."

"Elaine loved the Orpheum. She actually worked there for a while."

"Really? What'd she do?"

"Um, let me think. Mostly office stuff, bookkeeping and that. She quit right before Greg was born. She loved to go there for a special treat, though. We'd get a sitter, have dinner, and go to the show. The interior is pretty elaborate for a small town like Ozark."

"Yes, it is."

Mr. Ortman shot her a look. "How do you know? That building's been closed down since before you were born."

"Oh, er ... um, I just assumed. My mom's curator at the Ozark Museum. I help her out a lot 'cause I like old buildings, well, old stuff in general, and I know a little about architecture." She shrugged, hoping she hadn't spilled the beans on her friends and

gotten them all in trouble again. Not too lo.
ago, they'd snuck into the Orpheum and spen
an amazing night, but nobody else knew about
it.

"Well, I think it's a really sad thing to see.
Maybe there's something somebody can do to
stop it."

Sarah stared at the building, imagining the
giant neon sign lit and crowds of people
streaming through the door. She'd always felt
a connection to it and when they'd been inside
it was as if the Orpheum was thrilled that she
and her friends had discovered it. *Could a
building be happy? Sure, why not.* And Mr.
Ortman was right, somebody should do
something ... and that somebody was her. She
might not be able to stay in Ozark, but before
she left, she could at least save a beloved
landmark. The people she had to leave behind
deserved a chance to enjoy it.

"You know, you're absolutely right." She
stood up, excited for the first time since the

rrible news about moving to Chicago. "Thank you, Mr. Ortman! Thank you."

Sarah pecked the old man on the cheek, grabbed her bike, and pedaled toward the school. She and the Mud Street Misfits would save the Orpheum, and she wasn't going to let anything ... or anybody get in the way.

CHAPTER TWO

S arah saw her friends coming back from the cafeteria food line and waved them over.

"You look like a parrot," Connor said. He slapped his tray onto the table and sat opposite her. He'd pulled his tawny hair back into a tail and it suited the tie-dye Grateful Dead tee shirt he wore. She didn't understand the bears dancing across the front, but shrugged it away. That was Connor.

"Uh, thanks ... I guess," she said. "You look like a hippie."

"Excellent. That's what I was going for."

Liam slid in beside her, carefully opened his brown bag and neatly placed his PB&J and chips on a napkin.

Connor took a huge bite from the fried chicken sandwich he'd bought.

"Have you ever wondered what part of a chicken is completely round and the same size as a bun?" Sarah asked him.

Liam snorted.

Connor looked at the sandwich as he chewed. "No, actually. Must be the best part, though, 'cause this is exceptional."

Sarah opened her vintage Partridge Family lunch box and took out a Ziploc bag of carrots. "So, guys, I have some news."

"Yeah? Did someone get a pic of Bigfoot?"

"Connor ... stop. This is serious."

He held up a hand. "Sorry."

Liam looked at her with concerned eyes, a lank of thick black hair flopping down onto his forehead. "What is it? Are your moms okay? David?"

Sarah stared at her two best friends, throat tight and tears threatening. *How can I tell them?* They'd been so kind to her, reaching out when she'd first moved to Ozark. Since their adventure with Liam's new psychic ability and sneaking into the Orpheum to spend the night, they'd grown even closer. Finally, she took a big breath and blurted it out. "Mom-Rachel got a new job in Chicago, so we're moving."

Connor gaped mid-chew. "What?" he garbled around chicken and bun, a half-chewed chunk falling onto the table. "No way."

"Honestly, Connor. Your parents need to teach you some manners," Sarah said.

"Hippie, remember. No need for manners." He set the sandwich down and swallowed. "You can't move. We just started the Mud Street Misfits, and basically, you just got here."

"He's right. It's only been since fourth grade," Liam said.

Sarah nodded. "I know, and before that we were in Cincinnati, and before that, we were in California. This is the only place I've ever really thought of as home and I don't want to leave."

"What do your grandparents think of you moving all the time?" Liam asked.

Sarah shrugged. "Mom-Heather's folks died when she was in college, and I've never met Mom-Rachel's parents. She says they don't matter and we wouldn't like them, anyway."

"You've never met your grandparents?" Connor's eyes widened.

"Nope."

"This is awful," Liam said. "When did you find out?"

"Last night. I've felt sick ever since."

"What does David think about it?" Connor asked.

"He hates it." Sarah sighed. "I went to the museum this morning to talk to my mom about it. To try and change her mind, but..." Sarah shook her head. "I think Mom-Rachel has already accepted the job."

"This sucks," Connor said.

Liam nodded in agreement.

Sarah picked at her lunch and saw that her friends were doing the same. All the fun had gone out of the day.

"Boo-hoo. Geeky girl has to move away. Is she sad to leave Lurch and the Hobbit?" A scruff-covered pimply cheek appeared next to her, and Brandon's hand slithered out, grabbing the bag of carrots.

"What're you doing?" Sarah cringed. "Get away from me."

He slouched back and upturned the bag, spilling the carrots and then grinding them into the floor with his boot. "Oops."

"Here. Take Lurch's sandwich." Kaylee snatched the PB&J from in front of Liam, peeled apart the two pieces of bread, and tossed them peanut butter-side down into Sarah's lap. "There ya go. Eat up."

"Hey, cut it out." Connor stood up, and Dylan stepped in front of him. He was at least a head taller and stocky.

"Down, Hobbit." He said and shouldered Connor in the chest. He fell back against the table and sent his plate clattering to the floor.

The three laughed and slithered out the cafeteria door.

"At least you won't have to deal with those creeps in Chicago," Connor said, picking up the spilled chicken.

"They're horrible. Maybe I'll tell Principal Pete about them before I leave." Gingerly, Sarah peeled the bread off her pants and tossed the pieces onto Connor's plate with the chicken.

"Not a good idea." Liam shook his head. "You do that, and we'll be dead. They'll know exactly who ratted them out."

"I guess you're right, but somebody's got to do something."

"They're not dangerous, just stupid and mean. Eventually, we'll graduate and go away to college."

"Do you want me to get you guys more food? I've got some money."

"Nah. I wasn't really hungry anyway. I still can't believe you're leaving."

"Me either," Liam said.

"Yeah, well, I have an idea that might make us all feel better. It's a Mud Street Misfits thing."

"Yeah? Cool. It's time for another adventure."

The glimmer of excitement returning to Connor's eyes lightened her mood.

She folded her hands on top of the lunch box and leaned closer. "Guess who I saw at the museum this morning?"

"Uh ... your mom." Connor guessed.

"Well, of course, but also Mayor Scott. He was there to get some paperwork about the Orpheum."

"Really?" Liam straightened up in his seat. "What happened? Did you talk to him?"

"No, but my mom tried to talk him out of tearing the building down. He got really mad and gave her an earful. He was kinda mean."

"Wow," Liam said. "I've never seen him be nasty to an adult, just kids."

"I know, me neither. But when my mom mentioned finding another site for his condos, he really went off. Getting all huffy and like, 'We're going to tear down that eyesore.'

"After he left, I talked to my mom about it. She said that the city owns the building and can do whatever they want with it. The only way to keep it from being destroyed is to have it certified as a historic site. My mom won't do it because we're leaving, but I've got an idea.

"Meet me at our table in the park after school. Liam, bring Molly, and I'll get David. The Mud Street Misfits are going to save the Orpheum!"

***

"I can't believe you have to move away from Ozark," Molly said, dropping her backpack onto the picnic table and setting the volleyball at her feet. "When do you have to leave?"

"The end of the school year." Sarah put an arm around the younger girl's shoulders.

"That's only a few weeks away. What're you going to do?" Molly asked.

"There's not much I can do about moving away. We just need to make the most of the time David and I have left. And I want to do something important for Ozark before I leave. Are you guys up for another adventure?"

"Always," Connor said.

"Like what?" Molly perked up. She swept a neon green sweatband off her head and shook out her straight taffy-colored hair. "I don't know if anything could beat figuring out who the girl in the blue tie-dye shirt was and helping Liam with his new psychic gift, though."

"I agree. That was the coolest thing ever," Connor said.

"True," Sarah said. "But Mayor Scott wants to tear down the Orpheum and build condos on the site. That's wrong and I think we can keep it from happening. The building is old and beautiful, and it deserves to live on so others can enjoy it. All we have to do is get it certified as historic, and he won't be able to touch it."

"Stupid Mayor Scott wouldn't know an historic building if it dropped out of the sky and landed on him," Molly said.

"That's for sure," Liam said. "So, what do we need to do?"

"David read the notice, and it doesn't say when the demolition is going to happen, so the first thing is to find out the timing. I'm going to City Hall after school tomorrow to ask. Something like that has to be public information. Who wants to go with me? I could really use the moral support. If my throat closes up like it usually does, somebody'll need to do the talking."

"I'm in," Connor said. "I've never been in the city hall building."

"I can go," Liam said. "So long as we go after orchestra practice. The state band competition is coming up, and we're learning some really awesome new songs."

"Thanks. I knew I could count on you." With her friends gathered around the picnic table where they'd shared so many fun times, Sarah felt more like herself. The pain of having to leave this place and the people she loved ebbed a bit.

"During my free period, I did some Googling," she told them. "There're three main criteria for getting a building certified as historic: age, integrity, and significance." She ticked them off on her fingers. "It's definitely old enough. Integrity means that it mostly has to look like it did when it was built."

"It's a theater," Liam said. "Probably always has been."

"All in all, it looks like a plain old building," David said.

"No, it doesn't!" Sarah protested. She turned to study the old structure. "It's a very unique combination of Federal architecture with some Classic Revival elements. The sign was added later, like in the early 1900s. That's when neon was invented. That thing is huge, and the letters spelling out the name have to be two feet high. It would have looked amazing all lit up in red. It screams, 'Come on in and enjoy the show.'"

When she turned back, she met David's teasing blue eyes. She punched him lightly on the arm. "Don't do that. This is serious."

"So, significance must mean that it has to be connected to something really cool. Like a battle, or like where Betsy Ross sewed the American flag," Connor said.

"Right, and that's what we need to find. Proof that it was part of something important."

"Or that somebody famous had something to do with it," Liam added.

"Yes, that'd work, too."

"I'm sure lots of important stuff happened there," Liam said.

"Yes, but the problem is proving it. There are tons of stories about well-known people playing there when it was used for plays and performances but no *evidence* that it actually happened. There was a fire in one of the city's storage rooms in 1972. It burned up the old documents kept there. All of the support we could use to claim significance is gone. I think that's why the mayor was at the museum today. He was making sure there was no other information that would ruin his plans for condos. All that exists are some architectural drawings and purchase paperwork. Everything else was lost."

"I don't see how we can prove anything, then," Molly said. "Where would we start?"

"Remember the boxes we found in the Orpheum that night?" Connor said. "We need to search the whole place because there may be other stuff, but we should check those out first."

"That's exactly what I was thinking," Sarah said. "We need to go back inside ... now."

"Not tonight," David said calmly. "Dark soon."

* 35 *

"Yeah," Molly said. "And Liam and I are going to our dad's tonight. I called a family meeting to talk about adopting one of Sadie's pups."

"Molly, I told you. Dad will never go for it."

"I know, but I'm going to try anyway. That pup is so cute. I just want to hug him all the time. And, Connor's dad said we could have him."

"Yup," Connor agreed. "He's the last one, too. Tell your dad the pup's all alone now that his littermates are gone. Poor little guy."

"That's a great idea. Dad's a sucker for that kind of stuff."

"Well, it's your funeral." Liam shook his head.

"So, uh ... guys," Sarah said. "The Orpheum, remember. We need to go in this weekend."

Liam nodded. "If there's proof, that's where we'll find it."

"I'm not too sure about going back in there," Molly said. "It's really spooky. Full of cobwebs and creaky boards that sound like someone's sneaking up behind you. I'm pretty sure it's haunted. I can tell these things. I've heard the Mud Street Mare, you know."

"Before I found out about my psychic ability, I would have laughed at that, but now..." Liam ran a hand through his bushy black hair. "Maybe there is a ghost horse buried under Mud Street that roams at the full moon. All I know is that the night we were in there..." he nodded toward the Orpheum. "I kept thinking that someone was standing right behind me and was going to grab me any minute."

"Yeah, well. What about those two people who showed up in the middle of the night?" Connor said. "That was freaky."

"They must have come in through the front door, 'cause they sure as heck didn't come up the fire escape like we did," Sarah said.

"But there was a chain and padlock on the front, just like now," David reminded them.

"I was so freaked out, I thought I was going to hurl," Molly said.

"I thought you liked spooky stuff," Connor said.

"I do, but that place is pretty intense. What if those people are living there? What if they're ghosts ... or zombies?" Molly said.

"There is no scientific evidence that proves ghosts exist," David said.

"You don't believe in the supernatural?" Molly asked.

David shrugged. "I didn't say that ... exactly."

Sarah looked over her shoulder to where the Orpheum stood in the fading evening light. The giant double doors that marked the entrance were draped in caution tape, and the glass was smeared with decades of dust. She'd felt something in there, too, but it was nothing to be afraid of. Or at least, she hoped not.

"Well, whatever *is* in there needs to be preserved." She turned back to her friends. "So Saturday we go back in. Agreed?"

Relieved to see her friends nod, Sarah thrust out her fist and the others did the same.

"Save the Orpheum," she said, and they echoed her. As she looked around at their faces, she thought, *I'll take this moment with me when I leave.*

CHAPTER THREE

Sarah usually loved English class, especially now that they were studying *Romeo and Juliet*. They were on the first scene of Act III where Tybalt kills Mercutio, which was really cool, but her mind kept picturing the stacked boxes in the Orpheum, and she just couldn't pay attention.

When the bell rang, she raced to the computer lab. It was a free period, and she had fifty whole minutes to do some research on the old theater. Her first Google search brought up Orpheum theaters all over the country: Los Angeles, Memphis, Madison, Flagstaff, and the list went on and on. She clicked on a few of the links, but the buildings were all newer, built in the 1920s and part of a chain for showcasing vaudeville acts—not what she was looking for.

Okay, let's take a step back. Why are there so many theaters named the Orpheum?

She read, *The name 'Orpheum' for an entertainment hall comes from the Greek myth of Orpheus, whose music and poetry were so compelling that even the Gods were mesmerized. The word 'Orpheum' means 'house of Orpheus' or 'place of Orpheus'.*

Okay. That explains all the places with the same name. She narrowed her search to the Orpheum in Ozark, and one related article came up. *Yes! Now we're getting somewhere.*

The article was written in 2007, when the Orpheum turned one hundred and fifty years old. The author, Steve Lewis, had written mostly about the recent history of the building, but there were also some vague references to the past. It wasn't much, but she hit print anyway. Maybe it would help them in their search for proof.

***

Sarah gazed across at the park and watched the squirrels chase each other from tree to tree as if excited for the approaching spring. She thought about Chicago. It was a huge city, full of concrete and traffic—noise. Would they have to live in all that chaos? Ozark was surrounded by nature. Black Dog Ridge, with its thick forest and gigantic lake, was only an hour's drive away. She and David had camped there with Liam and his family tons of times. They even went to a cool summer camp near there. The counselors were really smart and knew about living off the land. They'd learned how to find edible plants and how to make shelter and start a fire. How could she leave all that?

The park blurred in her vision and she saw her house—cold, vacant. No shoes sitting helter-skelter in the entryway or hoodies draped over the furniture. All of her mom's treasures packed away, never to be displayed again. Empty rooms that echoed like long-forgotten tombs. A house was just a structure, it was the family living in it that made it a home. Just like the Orpheum. It was just a building unless someone cherished the memories that had been made there.

She wasn't crazy about going into City Hall and talking to strangers, but she had no choice. Ozark would be part of her past, but the Orpheum could still stand. She just had to speak up for it.

Her phone buzzed with a text from Liam.

where r u?

City Hall, front steps.

k, on our way.

A few minutes later, Liam and Connor rounded the corner on their bikes. She stood, brushing dirt from the seat of her teal-colored capris, and waited while they locked up.

"Sorry we couldn't meet at the school," Liam said as he climbed the steps toward her. "Practice ran over."

"Must've been another dress rehearsal." Sarah pointed to his tux.

"Yeah, I didn't have time to change."

She pulled the article from her pocket and showed them. "I found this when I Googled the Orpheum. It doesn't have a lot of information, but there's some general stuff."

"It says that during the '50s, some big-name groups performed at the Orpheum, but it doesn't list any of them," Liam said.

"I know. Frustrating. Well, you guys ready for this?" she asked, nodding toward the door.

"Absolutely," Connor said.

He sounded a lot more eager than she felt. Sarah just wanted to get the information they needed and get out of the building before Mayor Scott saw them.

"Okay, here goes."

She pulled open the heavy door, and they walked into a large foyer with polished marble floors and walls. The air was weighty and seemed to press in on her eardrums.

"Where do we go?" Connor whispered.

"There's a directory." She scanned the board, looking for the proper office.

"You kids need some help?"

The deep voice rumbled right behind her. Sarah spun around. A police officer stood with a cup of coffee in one hand and a rolled-up newspaper in the other. He was tall, burly, and completely bald, but his smile seemed friendly. She took a deep breath to calm her shaking nerves. "We're trying to find out when the Orpheum will be torn down. Do you know who we talk to about that?"

"Sure. You need to see Candice Blue in the community planning department. Her office is on the second floor. Just head up those stairs and turn left. You can't miss it."

"Oh, good. Thanks."

As she led them across the hall toward the staircase, Sarah felt like she should tiptoe. Though all three of them wore tennis shoes, it was as if their footsteps echoed in the open hall and disturbed the solemn nature of the building. Halfway up the stairs, Sarah's breath caught. Mayor Scott was coming toward her.

"What are you kids doing here?" His gaze ran over the three of them, seemed to puzzle over Liam's tuxedo and then settled on Sarah.

She could almost feel slime dripping off her face and a muscle in her cheek began to twitch. She wanted to run, but if she was going to save the Orpheum, she had to stand her ground. "We're ...uh ... here ..." Sarah had to swallow the lump in her throat before she could get the rest of the words out. "... to see Ms. Blue."

"What for?"

Connor stepped forward. "We're going to ask her when the Orpheum will be torn down, uh ... sir."

Mayor Scott straightened up, his pudgy belly straining the buttons on his jacket. "And why do you need that information?"

"Because we're going to stop it." Liam's voice was strong with confidence.

Thank goodness they're with me.

The mayor's face flushed a deep crimson. He took a step toward them, and Sarah couldn't stop herself from taking a step back.

"You're wasting your time. That's a done deal. The building is as good as gone, and that will be the best thing for this community. You would be better off playing on MyFace or Twitting. Whatever it is kids do these days." He brushed past them and continued down the stairs.

Connor made a fart noise, and the mayor whirled back.

"Which one of you did that?"

"Did what?" Connor asked.

Mayor Scott pointed a stubby index finger at them. "You three should be very careful." He turned and stomped out of the building.

Sarah smacked Connor on the arm. "What do you think you're doing? He already hates us. Don't make things worse."

"Yeah, I know. I just couldn't help myself. He's such a supercilious jerk."

"Supercilious?" Liam asked. "Another word of the day?"

"Yup. Last Wednesday's. Mom's used it twice so far. I think she likes it."

***

When they found Ms. Blue, Sarah had to suppress a giggle. The woman had blue tinged hair and wore a pale blue dress. For some reason it seemed hysterically funny and helped ease the tension Sarah felt. The woman stopped typing and looked up at them over blue framed glasses.

"May I help you?" Her church-mouse voice was barely audible over the fan running on the credenza behind her.

"Yes, Ms. Blue, my name's Sarah, and these are my friends, Liam and Connor. We would like to ask you a couple of questions about the Orpheum."

"Oh. Okay."

"We're wondering when it's scheduled to be torn down and if there's any way to stop it from happening."

Ms. Blue sighed, took off her glasses and motioned for them to sit down. "I'm afraid that is impossible. The mayor is pushing hard to have it demolished. I believe they're expecting the paperwork to clear soon, and demolition will start in two weeks."

"Two weeks? How could they do it so quickly?"

"Why do you want to stop it so badly?" Ms. Blue's curiosity gave Sarah hope.

"It's just that the building is so beautiful, and I'm sure it's contributed to the history of our town. It's sad to think of it being lost forever."

"Between us, I agree with you," Ms. Blue said. "I wish there was something I could do to help, but I'm afraid it's too late."

"That really sucks," Connor said.

"Yes, young man. It does."

"Well, I'm not going to give up," Sarah said. "We'll find a way."

"I wish you all the luck in the world but you're going up against a very powerful ... and difficult man." Ms. Blue slid a business card from a plastic holder on her desk and handed it to Sarah. "If there is anything I can do to help you, please let me know. I would like to see it remain the wonderful landmark that it is."

"Only two weeks," Liam said when they were back in the hallway. "We better find something fast."

"No kidding," Connor said. "It's a good thing we're doing our search tomorrow."

Sarah glanced around when she heard heavy footsteps coming their way. "Let's get out of here. I don't want to run into the mayor again."

***

Sarah twirled pasta onto her fork and reached for a chunk of bread. Dinner smelled amazing and she felt as if she hadn't eaten in a week.

"My intern, April, saw you at town hall this afternoon," Rachel said. "I assume the boys you were with were Liam and Connor?"

"Who?" Sarah spoke around the noodles in her mouth. "I've never met your intern. How would she know who I was?"

"She recognized you from the photo on my desk."

Sarah knew that tone. Even though her mom seemed calm, she was anything but. "We had to find out when the Orpheum is going to be torn down."

"What are they getting you into now?"

"Nothing, Mom. It's me. I want to save the Orpheum, and they're going to help me."

"Oh, Sarah," Heather said. "We talked about that. Even if you had time to go through the process of certification before we leave, I doubt it'd work."

"Besides, there's a lot to do to get ready for the move. I don't want you distracted by a frivolous game," Rachel said.

"It's not a game," Sarah insisted. "That building is very important to this town."

"No! I want you to concentrate on helping Heather go through all of the things in storage, selling or tossing what we don't want and packing the rest. I want to be ready to go right after school is out for the year. And I don't really want you spending time with those boys. They're dangerous!"

Sarah caught the look that passed between her moms, and realization struck her. "Is that why we're leaving Ozark? Because of what happened in Kenosha?"

"Of course not, honey. You know it's Rachel's new job."

Whenever there was tension in the house, Heather stepped in to calm the situation down. Sarah knew she meant well, but now she suspected there was more to the decision to move than just a job. *They want to take me away from my friends.* Slowly, she pushed her plate away and rose. "I'm not hungry anymore."

Sarah slammed the bedroom door as hard as she could. She'd get in trouble for it, but she didn't care. She hurled the napkin clenched in her fist across the room and threw herself onto the bed. With arms folded behind her head, she stared at the ceiling. The little bit of dinner in her stomach churned hotly, and tears streamed down her cheeks to collect in her ears. *They never listen to me. Don't care about what I want. No one ever has.*

The grainy, dog-eared photo was hidden under a notebook in the nightstand drawer. She studied the woman—girl really—who was shrouded in a dark hoodie and carrying a small bundle. This was the only image of her birth mom that Sarah had—a photo culled from the CCTV footage of the Santa Monica Public Library. That's where her mother had abandoned her, just left her like she wasn't important at all. She would never know her real mom, that was a certain and awful truth, but never knowing her heritage was worse.

She would never look into eyes that were her own or know that her mop of curly hair came from her grandmother—or great-grandmother... Sometimes she felt so separate, so alone. It made her feel as if she had no physical substance and was suspended above the earth by a tenuous thread that could be so easily snipped.

It didn't mean that she didn't love her moms. Of course, she did, and they loved her too, she knew that. She was grateful that they'd adopted her and given her a fantastic life. When Heather had become pregnant with David, Sarah had been excited about having a little brother and she loved him like crazy. But she also needed to feel as if she belonged somewhere. Ozark and her friends gave her that.

Gently, she put the photo back into its hiding place and slipped on her headphones. Her moms believed they were doing the right thing. *But they don't understand how much my friends and Ozark mean to me. It's my fault. I can never say what I really want to say.* She selected her favorite play list from the menu on her phone and let the music take her to another world.

CHAPTER FOUR

Sarah caught the scent of coffee and heard voices from the kitchen as she walked downstairs. David was setting the table, and Sarah's moms were at the stove. Physically, her moms were nothing alike—Heather, tidy and petite, Rachel, tall and rough around the edges--but they seemed to fit together. They were committed to each other and to creating a family. She knew it hadn't been easy for them and seeing them like this reminded Sarah of how much she loved them.

"Morning, sweetie," Heather said. "Egg casserole coming up."

It seemed that they'd chosen to ignore last night's scene, and Sarah was grateful. She would've accepted the punishment, knowing she deserved it, but she had important things to do today.

She kissed both her moms on the cheek. "Anything I can do to help?"

"Nope, we've got it under control."

Sarah slid into her chair next to David. "You ready for today?" she whispered.

He nodded and reached for the platter of casserole squares that Heather set on the table.

"Hey, save some for the rest of us," she teased as he forked three onto his plate.

"Just need some protein. Work day. Right, Sarah?"

"That's right." Rachel broke in. "I've got to go to the office, and Heather's going to the storage unit to look over what's there. I want you two to start in your rooms. Sort out what you want to take and what can be donated.

There are empty boxes in the garage if you need them."

"Uh, yeah. Sure." Sarah said, exchanging a look with David and knowing they'd be heading for the Orpheum as soon as their moms left.

***

They were supposed to rendezvous at the back of the building. By the time Sarah and David arrived, the others were waiting crouched along the bushes under the fire escape ladder.

"You're late," Connor said.

"How do you know? You don't even have a watch," Sarah said.

"I know because you're the last ones to get here, and we were on time."

"Yeah, okay, whatever. We had to wait until our moms left the house. We're supposed to be cleaning out our rooms. Getting ready for the move." She lifted her backpack. "I did make sandwiches for everyone, though."

"Nice! All is forgiven."

"Let's get in there and get started. We have an entire theater to search and not a ton of time," Sarah said.

Just like when they snuck into the Orpheum before, the fire escape ladder was too high to reach. Connor helped Sarah climb onto Liam's shoulders.

This time, she tugged it down gently and held on so it wouldn't return. They all clambered up the stairs to the metal landing.

"I hope we can get the door open again," Molly said.

Sarah hadn't thought of that. Last time it'd sort of opened on its own and they didn't have any way to lock it when they left. She gripped the knob, then grinned at Molly when it turned smoothly in her hand.

It took a few minutes for her eyes to adjust to the semi-darkness, but eventually the footprints from their previous foray into the building emerged on the dusty floor. The desk and chair arranged into the corner seemed to be layered more thickly in grime, and the cobwebs hanging from the ceiling and corners had grown thicker. The air was stagnant, heavy with the sour odor of mildew and scratchy with dust. But like before, Sarah felt that the building welcomed them.

A door slammed somewhere in the depths.

"What was that?" Molly shrank back against the door.

"Maybe it's whoever was here before," Connor said.

"We can see from the control room. Come on."

Sarah followed the bouncing beam of light from her phone as they ran down the hallway. The blankets were still scattered on the floor, and the cardboard soldier remained on guard in the corner. Sarah crossed to the large window that looked out over the auditorium.

"Kill the light," Liam whispered. "If anyone's down there, we don't want them to see us."

An ambient glow filled the space below, and Sarah was struck once again by the aged beauty of the old theater. Rows of once-plush seats were divided by dingy ruby-tinted carpet and swept down toward the stage. The raised hardwood planks had been polished to a shine by thousands of feet and lay barren, except for a single standing microphone placed prominently in the center. Intricately carved columns rose up on either side of the crimson-draped stage and ended in crown molding that had once been alive with colorful frescos. The remnants of a massive chandelier hung precariously from the soaring ceiling, and yards of handcrafted tapestry hung in shreds from the walls. How easily she could imagine the place full of people dressed up to enjoy a night out, eager to be transported, through music or play, to another world.

"I don't see anyone down there," David said, turning away.

"Nope. And I don't hear anything, either," Liam said.

"Must've been the wind," Connor said.

"Wind, schwind," Molly said. "It was a ghost. I told you the place is haunted."

Maybe, Sarah thought. *It's definitely eerie.* She took one more look across the auditorium, then started back down the hallway.

"Obviously, we have to go through all of these boxes," Sarah said, pointing to the pile in the corner of a storage room. "But we should search the other rooms first. I don't remember seeing anything else that night, but we were all focused on helping Liam."

"Let's split up. Some of us search, and some look through those boxes. It would speed things up," Liam suggested.

"Good idea. Why don't you take Connor and David and look around? Molly and I'll get started here."

***

Sarah tossed a handful of papers back into the last box she'd emptied and sighed. "I don't see anything that will help us." She swiped her dusty hands across her jeans.

"Yeah," Molly said. "Just old receipts and ledgers from when they used to show movies. And the ink is wearing off." She held her hands out to show Sarah the dark smudges. "We need to find something way older than this."

"Let's go see if the guys are doing better."

They walked to another room. The boys weren't there, but a ladder hung down from a hole in the ceiling, and voices sounded overhead.

"Cool, they found an attic," Molly said.

Excited, Sarah peered up through the opening, then had to step out of the way as Connor began to back down, manhandling one end of a heavy trunk. Liam held the other end, and together, with a lot of grunting, they maneuvered it to the floor.

"It's an old steamer trunk," Sarah said. She knelt down in front of it and ran her hands over the patinaed dark wood crisscrossed with brass-studded leather straps. "Probably turn of the century."

"Not that old, then," Connor said.

"1900, not 2000."

"Oh, yeah. That makes more sense."

"What's in it?" Molly asked.

"Dunno," Connor said. "There isn't a lot of room up there. Thought it would be easier to look through it down here."

Sarah lifted the lid and gasped. It was full of clothing. She reached down and lifted out an item curled on the top. Her hand arced high, and the red feather boa snaked through the air.

"Costumes?" Molly asked.

"Maybe. Let's take everything out and see."

"Awesome," Molly said, digging into the trunk and pulling out an armful.

"I think I'll stand back here and let them handle this," Connor said to Liam. "You know, the rats."

Molly shrieked and dropped everything on the floor. "Rats. Yuck!"

Sarah took a step back from the trunk and looked sharply at Connor. "Very funny."

"Liam said to watch out for them in the attic. I just figured…"

"Well, you could have said something earlier," Sarah said.

"I know." Connor smirked.

By the time they finished, clothing was piled around them and neatly sorted by type. A stack of hats included a military beret, a turban, and a lady's bowler with a veil. Besides the red boa scarf, they found three others in purple, pink, and silver. They nested together into a colorful pile.

Liam picked up a black suit coat from the pile of men's clothing. "This thing looks like it was made for a kid."

"It's a tuxedo jacket, but it's different from the kind you wear." Sarah ran a hand over the frayed satin lapel. "Back then, they were called tailcoats or tails. See how the front part is a lot shorter than the back? Probably from the '50s. It does look small, but that's because people were smaller back then."

"Yeah, my mom says we're bigger now 'cause of GMOs and growth hormones in dairy products. That's why I eat Twinkies. There's tons of that stuff in them, and I don't want to be a shrimp." Connor flexed a bicep. "Speaking of Twinkies, can we eat the sandwiches you brought now?"

"You're always starving," Molly said. She pointed to a black rotary dial phone at the bottom of the trunk. "What do you think that was doing with all the clothes? Seems a little strange."

"Yeah, but it's really cool. Too bad it doesn't work." Sarah picked it up and, trailing the three-foot frayed cord along the floor, walked toward the hallway. "Let's go eat in the control room and talk about what to do next."

She sank cross-legged onto the pile of blankets laid out on the floor and set the phone next to her. Unzipping her backpack, she passed out sandwiches.

"So have we found our first piece of evidence?" Molly asked.

"Nope," David said.

"He's right." Sarah sighed. "The trunk is old, and the costumes are amazing, but there's nothing there that gives the Orpheum any significance."

"All this, and we still haven't made any progress," Liam said. "That's discouraging."

"Heck, yeah," Molly said. "What do we do now?"

"I've been thinking about that and I think we should call Mr. Ortman," Sarah said. "A few days ago, I saw him sitting on a bench in the park. We talked, and I told him that the Orpheum was going to be torn down. He said his wife, Elaine, loved the old theater and actually used to work here."

"The girl in the blue tie-dye shirt worked here? That's cool," Connor turned to Liam. "Have you had any visions of her?"

"Nope. I really think she did what she needed to do and is gone. I haven't had any intense visions since then."

"This isn't a coincidence," Molly said. "It's gotta mean something."

"I agree," Connor said. "Maybe Mr. Ortman knows about an important event that happened at the Orpheum."

"It's worth a try," Liam said. "He gave me his number so I'll call him."

"Put him on speaker," Sarah said.

Liam nodded, and younger Greg Ortman's "Hello" reverberated in the dusty room.

"Hi, Mr. Ortman. This is Liam MacLeod. I don't know if you remember..."

"Sure, of course I remember you. How are you and your friends doing?"

"We're doing fine. As a matter of fact, they're here, and I have you on speaker."

"Hey, that's great. Hi, everyone. I'm glad you called... It's actually perfect timing. My dad's been showing me a ton of pictures from around the time he bought that album. You know, the Allman Brothers one."

"That's awesome."

"Yeah, it really is. It's as if that album flipped a switch in my dad. He's had a great time going through old pictures and reliving the memories."

"Hi, Mr. Ortman. This is Sarah. We'd really like to talk to your dad about the Orpheum. Have you heard that it's going to be torn down?"

"Yes, actually. He mentioned that you'd told him. That's why it's amazing that you called today. My dad just showed me a couple of pictures of my mom standing in front of the old theater. She's with an older lady that she worked with."

"Wow. Does your dad know who the other lady is?" Liam asked.

"Hold on just a sec. I'm going to get him so he can tell you what he knows."

They heard a clunk as the phone was set down, then faint voices talking in the background. Sarah looked excitedly around at her friends, holding up crossed fingers on both hands.

"Okay, he's here. I'm going to put you on speaker."

"Hey, kids." The older man's voice sounded loudly, and a whine of feedback shot from Liam's phone.

"Dad, you don't have to get that close. They can hear you."

"Oh, okay. Is that better?"

"Hi, Mr. Ortman. This is Sarah. Liam, Molly, Connor, and David are here, too."

"Good, good. Hi, kids. Greg says to tell you about the pictures I found of Elaine at the Orpheum. What do you want to know?"

"We're doing research on the building, trying to get it declared a historic site. We need to find out if the Orpheum was part of something important."

"I'm surprised that wasn't done years ago."

"I know. It probably would've been, but all the documentation was lost in a fire," Sarah told him.

"I don't really know too much about it. Elaine loved that place and her job there, but they just showed movies and the occasional local play, nothing historic or significant."

"You found some photos? Your wife and another woman?" Liam asked.

"Yup. They're standing in front of the building by the main door. I'm pretty sure it was her last day of work. That's why I took the photos. She was so pregnant she could barely stand up, and she was wearing that old tie-dye shirt I told you about."

"What about the other lady in the pictures? Do you know who she is? We'd like to find her and ask about the Orpheum."

"Um, I don't recall right off. I know she'd worked there for a long time. Elaine really liked her ... kind of a mother figure for her."

"Do you want me to text you copies of the photos?" the younger Greg Ortman asked.

"That would be great. Thanks. And if you think of anything else, let us know."

Liam tapped *end* on his phone and shoved it back into his pocket. "It's too bad he can't remember the lady's name."

"Yeah, it really is." Sarah sighed.

"Another dead end," Connor said.

"Is there anywhere else in the building we can look for records?" Molly asked.

"I don't think so. We've looked in every room and closet."

"Liam could try touching all of the clothes to see if he gets any visions," David suggested.

"I think I did handle most of them. The only thing I got was a general feeling of tension combined with excitement. No clear images of anything or anyone."

"Remember, Cora said that energy attached to objects is stronger when a trauma or significant event occurred. She said it was like an energy fingerprint left behind," Molly said. "There must not have been anything special that happened to the costumes or the people wearing them."

Sarah knew that Cora had helped Liam a lot when they'd been trying to figure out what his visions were all about. She'd never met Cora because she'd been working with her mom the day her friends had gone to the shop. Molly had told her all about it though. The shop was filled with tons of strange woo-woo stuff and Cora had given everyone a stone that was supposed to have powers that would help them.

"The phone." David suggested. "Sarah took it out of the trunk and brought it in here. You haven't touched it."

"I'll give it a try." Sarah nudged it over to Liam. He hesitated and then settled his hands onto the phone, closing his eyes.

The stillness of the room seemed to thicken as if the building held its breath. Even Connor stopped eating. Finally, Sarah couldn't take it any longer.

"What do you see?"

Liam blinked a couple of times, then lifted his hands. "Wow, that was interesting."

"Well, spill it, dude," Connor said.

"Okay, okay. I'm trying to organize it in my mind. The first thing I saw was a lady's face. It was like right here." He held a hand about six inches from his nose. "She floated there for a few moments and then faded away."

"What did she look like? Describe her."

"Um, old. Maybe Dad's age."

Molly snorted. "Don't let him hear you say that."

"Yeah," he grinned. "Anyway, she had blue eyes and gray hair, kinda frizzed. She was smoking a cigarette that looked like a skinny cigar."

"Gross," Molly said. "Regular cigarettes are bad enough, but a cigar?"

"Did she say anything?" Connor asked.

"Nope, just smiled and faded away. Next, I saw the stage downstairs. It was empty except for a stool and microphone. Now that I think about it, the mic was just like the one we found backstage. A spotlight shone on both things." He shrugged. "That was it. The next thing I heard was Sarah's voice."

Liam's text message alert beeped.

"Uh-oh," Molly said. "Is it Mom?"

Liam shook his head. "No, it's a text from Mr. Ortman with an image attached." He retrieved and then enlarged the photo. "No way."

"What?" The others chorused.

He turned the phone around so they could see the photo that Greg Ortman had sent.

Two women—who could have been mother and daughter—stood with their arms around each other's waists. One wore capris and a blue tie-dye shirt over a very pregnant belly and the other wore a brown pleated skirt and white blouse. Both were smiling, but you could see a tinge of sadness in their eyes. The massive marquee of the Orpheum was an impressive backdrop.

"This is the lady I saw when I touched the phone."

"Wow. And that's the girl from your visions. You've seen both of them. Dude, you *do* see dead people."

"Oh, for goodness sake," Sarah said. "It's not like that." She turned to Liam. "Is it?"

Liam shrugged. "Not like in the movie, anyway. But just like when I first saw the girl in the tie-dye shirt, I don't have a clue what it means."

"It means that this woman is important," Sarah said.

"According to Mr. Ortman's text, her name's Audrey Lewis. It was written on the back of the photo, along with the date."

"Oh, my gosh." Sarah gasped. "This is so cool! We have another lead to follow. Not a dead end, after all."

CHAPTER FIVE

Sarah grabbed her phone and typed *Audrey Lewis, Ozark* into the Google search bar. Her friends surrounded her and watched over her shoulder. Several hits came up, but nothing that looked like it would connect to the Audrey Lewis they were looking for.

"Try Audrey Lewis and the Orpheum," Liam suggested.

Sarah's fingers flew over the tiny keyboard. She tapped *go* and studied the available choices. "A lot of Audreys, and a lot of Orpheums, but nothing with them combined."

"Add Ozark and see what happens."

She did and frowned when the top hit was a reference to the same article she'd found before. "We already know that article wasn't much help. This is getting frustrating. How about..."

"Wait," Liam said. "Pull up that article again."

"What? Why?"

"Just do it. I think I know what the connection is."

Sarah shrugged and clicked on the reference to the article. She scanned the first few words and gasped. "Lewis! The author's Steve Lewis! Audrey Lewis! That has to mean something."

"Woo-hoo," Molly cried.

Sarah typed in *Steve Lewis*, added *Ozark* and the *Orpheum,* and hit *search.* The link for the article came up again along with information on fifteen people in the area with the name Steve Lewis.

"How do we narrow this down?" Connor asked.

"We're going at this all wrong," Sarah said. "Instead of starting with this long list, why don't we call the place that published the article? Maybe they would give us Steve Lewis' number or tell us how to contact him."

"Great idea," Liam said.

They pulled the article back up and found that it was written for *The Ozark Trail*, a monthly magazine.

"Our moms get that magazine," David said.

"Look up the phone number," Connor said.

"Already there," Sarah said.

"Call it."

"What do I say?"

"Try the truth," David spoke up. "We're trying to save the Orpheum and want to find out as much information as we can. We saw the article Steve Lewis wrote and want to ask him some questions."

"What the heck, it just might work," Connor agreed.

"Okay."

She called the number and told their story. "Yes, if you have his phone number that would really help." She made writing motions with her hand.

Liam dug a pen and pad of paper out of his backpack and passed it over to her.

"Yes, I'm here." She quickly scribbled a number. "Thank you so much. You've been a big help." She touched *end* and turned to the group. "The lady I talked to was really nice. She said that he hadn't written for them in years, but she gave me the last phone number they had."

"Awesome," Connor said. "Hopefully, it still works."

Sarah keyed in the number, and a male voice answered.

"Hello, I'm looking for Mr. Steve Lewis, who wrote an article about the Orpheum several years ago. It was published in *The Ozark Trail* magazine. Are you that Steve Lewis?"

"Uh, yes. Why do you want to know?"

"Well, my friends and I are trying to save the Orpheum." Sarah rushed on, explaining everything. "The only thing we can think to do is to get it listed as a historical site, and that requires facts that tie it to a significant historical event. So far, we haven't found any. We thought that because you wrote that article, you might know something that could help us."

"I had no idea they were going to tear it down. That's a great old building. Tell you what. I'm sure I still have my research related to that article. I tend to keep things like that. I'll pull it out and see if I have anything that would help. Can I call you back tomorrow?"

"Yes, absolutely."

"Can't make any promises, but I'll look."

"Thank you. Really," Sarah said and ended the call. "He's going to check his files and call me tomorrow."

"Cool," Liam said. "Sounds like we're done for today, then."

"I guess you're right." Sarah sighed.

"Hey, what's wrong?" Connor asked.

"It's just that we have so much to do in such a short time," Sarah said. "It bugs me to have to wait."

"Yeah." Liam awkwardly patted her on the back. "But we've made some progress, too."

"That's for sure," Molly said. "Best of all is that we found those cool costumes. I hope we can keep them."

"If we can, then my Halloween costume is all set," Connor said. "I'm wearing that cool black suit jacket and being a vampire." He grinned ghoulishly, making Sarah laugh.

She jumped when her phone rang. "It's Steve Lewis. Maybe he found something." She answered and nodded several times as she listened. "We'll be there." She ended the call and looked at her friends. "He found the box of information. He's going to be home tomorrow morning and says we can come and get it."

"Yes! We're back in business." Connor held his hand up in a high five, and Sarah slapped it.

"Are you crazy?" Molly said. "Go to a strange man's house? I don't think so. He could be an axe murder with a dozen kids buried in his backyard."

"Oh, for gosh sakes. You've been watching too many of those British murder mystery shows with your mom," Sarah admonished. "He lives about three blocks from here, and he's not a serial killer." Sarah gave her friends a shriveling look. "I'm going. You can come or not, I don't care."

"Of course we'll go with you," Liam said.

"It's getting late and will be dark soon," David said. "Moms are probably home by now."

She knew he was right. But another day had passed, and now the move and the demolition were one day closer.

They all walked back to the office and Sarah set the black phone on the corner of the desk.

Connor cracked open the door. He stuck his head out and then pulled it back in. "The coast is clear."

Molly stopped before stepping through the door. "Do you smell cigarette smoke?"

Sarah sniffed. "No, why?"

"Nothing, probably." She shrugged. "Just thought I smelled something funny."

"Probably Connor's tennis shoes."

"Oh, yuck."

Sarah looked around the office one more time, then did a double take when her gaze passed over the phone. She stared at the instrument and then finally shook her head. For a moment, she thought she'd seen a faint cloud of smoke hovering above it.

***

Rachel jerked the door open before Sarah could use her key. "Where have you been?"

"Well, geez," Sarah said and brushed past her.

"Library," David said.

Sarah sent him a grateful look knowing she would owe him one because David didn't like to lie.

"Good timing," Heather called brightly from the kitchen. "Dinner's almost ready. Go wash up."

On her way to the powder room, Sarah saw the unspoken communication pass between her moms. *Uh-oh, what now?* She knew that look, and it always meant something was coming. *Have they decided to leave sooner?* She gripped the edge of the sink. The joy of being with her friends and the hope that had sprung up with finding Steve Lewis faded. *I hate this! I have absolutely no control over my life.* Her mother called again, and Sarah sighed. *Time to face the music.*

Knowing her moms had expected them to sort through their stuff today, Sarah thought she'd be bombarded with a talk about responsibility and fulfilling family obligations. About setting a good example for her younger brother and the old standby of, "How can we trust you?" But instead, Heather chattered on about what she'd found in the storage unit as if she'd actually be able to keep her treasures.

What is wrong with you? Sarah wanted to shout. *Don't you realize all that stuff is as good as gone? There's no way we'll be able to take all that stuff to Chicago.*

She looked at the chicken strips on her plate. They were her favorite, and she knew it was her mom's way of trying to make things better, but the sight of them made her want to gag. Despite finding Steve Lewis and the possibility he might have some information that would help, she wondered if they'd really be able to get the certification done in time. No matter how she rearranged what they'd found out about the Orpheum in her head, failure was the result. Her dream of leaving something of value behind when she left dissolved into a blur of disappointment. She hadn't just failed the beautiful theater—she'd failed herself. No one in Ozark would ever remember that she'd been here.

"So..." Heather said, "we have exciting news."

Sarah raised her head to see her moms clasp hands.

"I heard from the Chicago firm today," Rachel said. "They confirmed the job offer and even arranged for us fly out to look for housing."

"I already started looking online," Heather said. "Sarah, I found an adorable 1950s Craftsman-style three-bedroom that I know you'll love. It's very close to a park. The bus ride to school won't be that long, either."

Sarah knew she should say something. Tell Mom-Rachel congratulations, maybe ask to see the online listing, but the kind words wadded in her throat, and the mean ones ached to get out. Tears stung her eyes, and she looked at David, hoping he would help.

"So, anyway," Rachel said into the silence that greeted her announcement. "We're going to take a quick trip up to look."

"We don't have to go, do we?" David asked.

"Oh, well..." Heather glanced at Rachel. "I guess not. I'll see if Mrs. Miller can stay over."

Sarah couldn't hold back any longer. "Good, 'cause I don't care about the stupid Craftsman." She met Heather's eyes defiantly and ignored the hurt she saw there.

"Young lady..." Rachel said. "You apologize right now. I don't know why you're being so difficult. We're only doing what's best for this family."

"What's best?" Sarah stood. "That's not true at all. If you cared about us ... about me, you'd listen to what we want. You only care about what you want ... your stupid career." Sarah grabbed her plate and marched into the kitchen. She tossed the uneaten chicken into the trash.

***

The Orpheum screamed in anguish as the giant steel jaws ripped its brick skin apart.

"No, no!" Sarah cried, rushing forward, stumbling over chunks of debris that steamed like severed limbs. The air was thick with dust and smoke, acrid and sticky. It held her back as she tried to get between the giant machine and the building she had sworn to protect. She pushed forward, clawing her way through the dense air. Finally, she stood in front of the gaping maw of the beast, screaming, arms out as a human barrier to the inevitable destruction. The behemoth growled and shook its gigantic head. The steel monster rolled forward relentlessly and, as it neared, scooped her into its black abyss.

Sarah tore herself from the dream, a scream squeaking from her lips. Her throat felt raw and her eyes gritty, as if from the lingering sting of dust and smoke. The enduring stink of scorched plaster permeating her room. She sat up in bed and folded her arms protectively around her legs. *Oh, my gosh. Oh, my gosh.* She shook her head, but couldn't forget the horror of watching the building be torn apart. The clock on her nightstand flashed *11:11* and illuminated a dim figure that slowly emerged from the dark corner by the door. "David? What're you doing here?"

"Not David." A woman's raspy voice whispered. She drifted to the bed. Gray hair formed a spiky halo around her head and smoke curled from a slender brown cigarette that wobbled between her lips. She took a sharp drag, blew the smoke out her nostrils, then pinched the cigarette between her thumb and forefinger. "But you know who I am. Don't you?"

Sarah stared at her, closed her eyes, then opened them again. The woman was still there. *I must still be asleep, dreaming. It's the stress, that's it. I'm going to lie back down and forget about this.*

"Who am I, Sarah?" the woman insisted.

"You're ... uh ... you're Audrey," Sarah stammered. "But that's not possible."

"Oh, hon! Of course it is." Audrey cackled. "You think all the stories about ghosts are bunk?" She sat on the edge of the bed. "Listen, I don't have a lot of time. I could be yanked back soon. We just wanted to thank you for what you're doing for the Orpheum. You'll find what you need if you..."

Sarah's ears popped, and Audrey disappeared. *What the heck just happened?* Sarah threw back the covers and switched on her lamp. The room was empty, and she was alone, just as she should be. The clock now read 5:29, which made more sense, because the sky was lightening outside her window. There was a lingering odor of cigarette smoke, but even that was fading quickly.

I'm awake. I'm sure of it. Sarah pinched the skin on the back of her hand just to make sure. *Yup, that hurt.* Had the ghost of Audrey Lewis just been in her bedroom? *This is too crazy for words.* "Or ... maybe not," she whispered, gazing around the room. Liam would know what it meant and she couldn't wait to talk to him.

CHAPTER SIX

By 7:30, Sarah couldn't wait any longer. She grabbed her phone. *Meet me at our table in the park ASAP*, she texted to Liam and Connor. *Bring Molly.*

what's up??? Liam's return text came back instantly.

need to tell you something. critical.

on the way.

me, too. Connor responded.

***

The bright morning sun and the everyday sound of birds singing made what Sarah had to tell them even stranger. She spilled it out in a rush. "You know, a few months ago, I would have dismissed the whole thing and never thought about it again. But ever since Liam started having visions, I guess I'm a lot less skeptical that these things can happen," Sarah said.

"So you think it really was Audrey's ghost?" Molly asked.

Sarah shrugged. "It looked like her picture, kinda. It sure was weird, but it didn't really freak me out ... at least, not too much."

"What's the point of having a ghost visit you if they don't help?" Connor shook his head. "I mean, she was right there and still didn't tell you where to find the proof we need."

"I think communication's hard for them," Liam said. "The girl in the tie-dye shirt couldn't tell me what I needed to know, either. It would have been a lot easier if she'd just come out with it at the beginning."

"Maybe Audrey will come back and give you more info," Connor said.

"Yeah, we sure need something. Let's go see if Steve Lewis can help us."

The house was a small bungalow a few blocks off the town square. Sarah marched up the porch steps and rang the bell. She didn't know what Steve Lewis looked like, but she expected he would be older, maybe Mr. Ortman's age.

Instead, a man who seemed a little younger than her moms answered the door. He was dressed neatly in tan chinos and an evergreen golf shirt. The smile he gave Sarah made his eyes dance.

He held the door open for them. "You must be Sarah."

"Yes. Hi, Mr. Lewis. This is my brother, David, and our friends Liam, Molly, and Connor. We're working together to save the Orpheum."

"Well, come on in. I'm really happy to meet you all and to know that you're doing something for the old theater."

He led them to the kitchen table, where a small box sat. "This is everything I have on the Orpheum. You're welcome to it."

Is that all there is? Determined to stay positive, Sarah started to pull off the lid but stopped as Steve did the same. "Oh, sorry,"

"No, it's okay." He smiled. "You go ahead."

She snatched the lid off the box, reached inside, and lifted out a spiral notebook, some small audio tapes, and one photograph with a yellow sticky note attached to it. It said *Grandma, Margret, and Lilly.* The photo was black and white and showed three girls, probably high school age, standing in front of the Orpheum. She set it carefully on top of the notebook.

"I was still in college when I wrote that article, and really excited that the theater was one hundred and fifty years old. I always loved that place. I started my research by interviewing my grandmother, because she'd worked there for years. The stories she told were amazing. Then, when I tried to verify what she said, I couldn't find anything to back it up. There was a fire that destroyed most of the paperwork and pictures."

"We heard about that," Sarah said.

"My grandmother remembered quite a bit about the Orpheum, but at the time, she was starting to lose her memory—Alzheimer's—so that made verification even more iffy. When I wrote the final article, I decided to leave out a lot of the information she gave me because I was worried it might not be true." He tapped the picture. "The other two girls were my grandma's best friends. I had a chance to meet them when I was younger. What a kick they were. They may be still alive, I don't know. The notebook has all of my notes, and the tapes are recordings of my conversations with Grandma. There's about two hours' worth."

"What types of things did she talk about?" Liam asked.

"Well, she said that she'd heard the theater was used as a hospital during the Civil War."

"Wow, really?" Molly asked.

"I've heard the hospital story before. There's nothing to prove it, though," Sarah said.

Steve nodded. "She also said she saw Elvis and Johnny Cash perform there, before they became big stars."

"What?" Sarah gasped. "That's great."

"I know, but the issue is proof. There just doesn't seem to be any. And, like my grandmother, the folks who saw anyone perform at the theater in its prime are gone."

"Proof." Sarah sighed. "It always comes back to that, doesn't it?"

"Well, who knows. Maybe you'll find something that I didn't. Either way, I know my grandma would be very happy that you're trying to save that beautiful building."

"I'm sorry that she got Alzheimer's," Molly said.

"Yeah, me too." He turned away slightly, looking at the notebook and tapes. When he looked back, he was smiling. "But she lived a wonderful life. Had a lot of fun and was a lot of fun. She would have loved meeting you all and probably would be trying to save the

Orpheum herself. I just wish I had more information to give you."

Sarah thought about her early morning visitor and silently agreed with Steve. She put the notebook and tapes back in the box. "Thanks for loaning this to us. We'll return it when we're done."

"No hurry. It's just been gathering dust in my office," Steve replied. "If you run into anything that you have a question about, please feel free to give me a call. And if you get the chance to go in and look around the Orpheum before it's gone, do it. It's an amazing place."

"Er ... yes. That would be fun to do." Sarah could feel a blush creeping up her cheeks.

An awkward silence settled, and finally Liam said, "Well, thanks again for your help."

Once they were back on the sidewalk, Connor said, "Maybe we can find out who Margret and Lilly are. If they're still alive, we can talk to them about the Orpheum."

"Yes, but I just don't think stories are going to be enough. We need to find hard facts," Sarah said.

"Let's start with the tapes and see if there's any information on them we can use to dig deeper," Liam said.

"Did you see the size of them? They're, like, miniature. I doubt there's a way to play them," Molly said.

"It's a microcassette. Mom-Rachel has a player," David said.

"She does?" Sarah gaped at him.

"Yup. It's in her desk drawer."

"Sweet!" Connor said. "Can you get your hands on it? Like ... now?"

"Sure."

"We should listen to the tapes at the Orpheum," Molly said.

"You're right. That's the perfect place." Sarah turned to David. "Get the recorder, and we'll meet you in the back of the Orpheum. Don't get caught."

"Yeah, right." He laughed and sped off on his bike.

***

They settled on the blankets piled on the floor of the control room. Sarah set the notebook on the floor beside her and inserted the tiny tape marked with the number one into the machine.

Steve Lewis's voice filled the room as he started off the conversation. "For the record, what is your full name?"

"Oh, Stevie, you know who I am."

A gust of wind blew in through the open doorway of the control room bringing in the distinctive odor of cigarettes. It rustled the pages of the notebook, fanning it open and sending the picture rolling across the floor. Connor made a grab for it and missed. His effort was met with a low rumble of laughter that echoed in the room.

"Did you hear that?" Sarah asked.

"I did. What was it?" Molly asked.

"The wind," Connor said. "Made a funny noise."

Liam looked at Sarah. "I don't think it was the wind. There aren't any open doors or windows in this building."

Sarah nodded.

"What do you mean," Molly said, scooting closer to Sarah.

"I think it was the Orpheum ... or rather whatever lives here. They like hearing Audrey's voice." Sarah switched the player back on.

"I know, Grandma, but this is for that article I told you about, so you have to say it."

"Well, all right." She sighed loudly. "Audrey Elizabeth Lewis."

"When and where were you born?"

"Why do I have to tell you that? I don't want just anybody knowing how old I am."

"It's okay, Grandma. Probably no one will hear this but me."

"You already know how old I am."

"It's for the record, Grandma."

Sarah smiled at the hint of frustration in Steve's voice.

Audrey sighed again. "All right. I was born right here in Ozark on December 23, 1937."

As Sarah listened, she skimmed through the notebook. She could tell the notes followed the conversation Steve and his grandmother were having. Audrey was talking about her first date. She was sixteen and went to see a local band play at the Orpheum.

"Oh, it was such fun. I just love music and dancing."

Sarah didn't recognize the name of the band, but she highlighted it in Steve's notes as something to Google later. As the conversation continued, Steve asked his grandmother if she'd heard any special stories about the Orpheum.

"Oh yes. Everyone knows it was used as a hospital during the Civil War."

"I didn't know that, Grandma."

"Well, you must not have been paying attention in history class, Stevie. The battle of

Black Dog Ridge happened just down the road. The injured soldiers from both sides were brought into town. They used the schoolhouse at first, but there were just too many of those poor boys who were hurt, and they had to expand into the Orpheum.

"One of my friends, Margret, her grandpa was a medic. He worked there, trying to help those young men. She has his old medical bag and showed me some of the instruments he used." She made a sound of disgust. "Oh, they looked wicked."

Sarah knew that the town had used the schoolhouse for a hospital, and that building was already certified as a historic site. There was an old medical bag on display at the museum, and she wondered if it was the same one.

Connor pushed the pause button. "The grandma seems like she would've been fun to know."

"A little spacy, though," Molly said.

They all nodded, and Sarah started the tape again.

"Grandma, do you remember any big performing groups or entertainers coming to the Orpheum?"

"Well, there was the time I got to sing with Elvis. Is that what you mean?"

"Elvis? Elvis Presley?"

"Of course, Elvis Presley." Audrey's laugh brightened the control room. "Is there another one? I saw him and sang with him."

"Grandma, that's amazing. You never told me about that. What happened?"

"He and another gentleman. I can't quite recall his name. Joe ... Jasper ... maybe John ... anyway, something like that, came to town. It was probably '54, maybe '55. I was seventeen or eighteen, can't remember for sure. We knew they were going to be here for a show that night because there were posters all over, and the Orpheum had their names on the marquee. It cost a dollar fifty to see the show, and we didn't have that kind of money, but

Lily, Margret, and I had a plan. Lily knew the boy who ran the spotlights, so she thought she could get us in. Turned out to be a pretty small crowd, so we didn't have any trouble."

"But how did you sing with him?"

"Those boys put on quite a show, even though their backup singers never got here. Near the end, the other man, John Cash—that was his name, left the stage, and Elvis said he was going to sing some gospel songs. He said that God heard his songs best when they were shared and asked if anyone wanted to sing along. My friends and I jumped at the chance and ran up onto the stage. There was only one microphone, so Elvis sat on a stool, and we clustered around him. Margret told me later that he patted her bottom, but I think she was fibbing. He was such a nice young man; I don't think he would have done something like that."

"Do you remember any of the songs he sang or that you sang with him?"

There was a pause on the tape, then Audrey said, "What?"

"Elvis Presley, do you remember any of the songs you sang with him?"

There was another long pause. "Who is Elvis Presley?"

"What? No." Sarah smacked her fist on her thigh then punched the pause button on the player.

"No wonder he didn't use any of her stories," Molly said.

"Yeah, they were probably all made up," Connor agreed.

They listened to the tape for a few more minutes, then Sarah shut it off.

"We're not going to find anything here." Gently she placed the photo inside the notebook and slid everything into her backpack. "We only have a few days left, and I don't know what else to do."

"You're not looking at this the right way," Liam said. "What about that thing with the

Orpheum and the Civil War? If we can prove that, we've got it nailed."

Sarah shook her head. "I have personally cleaned, arranged, and re-arranged every artifact that this town has regarding the Civil War, and I've never seen any reference to the Orpheum."

"Maybe you missed something?" Connor said.

"Yeah," Molly said. "When you were doing work for your mom, you probably weren't thinking about the Orpheum. That would've been before all this started."

"I just don't know, guys. I suppose I could ask my mom. Maybe she knows something and doesn't realize it." She sighed deeply and could almost feel the fabric of her life shred as her world fell apart around her. "Come on. Let's go down to the stage. Maybe something will come to me."

***

The old microphone sat center stage. It looked lonely and abandoned. Sarah placed a hand on it as if offering comfort. She looked out over the rows of seats flanked by aisles carpeted in dirty red. "I just know that people loved to come here and enjoy a show or listen to amazing music. It makes me sick that Mayor Scott wants to destroy it just so he can make some money. It's not right."

"No, it's not," Liam said. He unfolded a seat in the front row. A puff of dust blossomed around him when he sat.

"We're doing everything we can," David said. He lounged in the row in back of Liam, butt in one seat, feet in another.

"This place is just so cool. I bet these velvet drapes were beautiful when they were new." Molly ran a hand down them, setting them swaying. "Hey, I know. Sarah, why don't you sing? Your voice is beautiful, and it was amazing when you did it before. Maybe it'll help you come up with an idea."

"Excellent idea," Connor said. "We'll be your adoring fans." He took the seat next to Liam.

"No, that's silly."

"It's not," Liam said. "Take advantage of the acoustics in here while you have the chance."

Sarah looked out at her friends. They seemed sincere, and Liam was right. This could be the last time they'd ever be in here. "Well ... I guess." She thought for a moment, and the perfect song came to her.

The sound of her quiet voice in the vast auditorium seemed so trivial. She broke off. "I can't do this. I feel ridiculous."

"No, Sarah. Don't stop. I love 'Fight Song'. It's been around forever but it's my favorite," Molly cried.

"Yeah, go for it," Connor encouraged.

Sarah took a deep breath and started again. By the time she got to the chorus, new determination to save the building flooded her heart.

The Orpheum is my fight. But it's more than just saving the building. It's about being heard, being cared about and sharing this time with my friends. She thought about the stories Molly had told her about Cora. She'd helped Liam and maybe she could help her too. She had questions and Cora may be the only one with the answers.

Her friends were on their feet hooting, fists pumping. They picked up the beat and clapped along as Sarah sang the final lines.

Sarah felt the electricity in the air and knew it was more than just the excitement of the song. Over the auditorium, a shimmer of mist grew. It started where her friends danced and rolled backward across row after row. The seats lost definition, as if flickering between this world and another. Silvery light sparked within the haze and merged into the faces of men and women applauding in silent appreciation.

As the song ended, Sarah watched the spectral images recede into the darkness. She jumped off the stage, and her friends gathered around. "Guys, that was so cool. I think I actually saw people in the audience."

"Really?" Molly whipped around.

"I don't know about that, but your song was awesome," Connor said. "'Fight Song' is our Sarah in a nutshell. You never give up."

The truth of what he said struck her. *Our Sarah. I'm theirs ... and they're mine. That will never change, no matter where I live.*

"I know what we need to do next," Sarah said. "We need to talk to Cora."

"Cora? Why?"

"Liam, you said she helped you a lot when you didn't know what to do about your visions."

"That's true. She really did," Liam said.

"And she gave us crystals. She'll know exactly the right one for you, Sarah," Molly said.

"I don't know if a rock can help me save the Orpheum, but I'm willing to find out. Let's go see her."

CHAPTER SEVEN

They walked into Cora's Crystal shop to find the proprietress sitting on a purple mat with her long legs crossed and her eyes closed. She was thin with silver hair pulled back in a long braid. Beaded earrings hung from her ears and copper-colored bracelets glinted on her forearm. The music of wind chimes swaying in the breeze filled the space.

Cora opened one eye, looked at them, and closed it again. "Hmmm. I thought that door was locked."

"Maybe we should come back another time," Sarah whispered to Liam.

"No, no," Cora rose and stretched her arms upward, twisted side to side, then bent over at the waist and shook her hands. Finally, she straightened. "Not as young as I used to be." She gestured to the door. "Don't usually have customers this early, so I thought I'd get my meditation done. Looks like the Universe had different plans for me."

"Cora, we're sorry to interrupt, but Sarah needs a crystal," Molly said.

"Oh?" When Cora turned her deep blue gaze on Sarah, she felt as if the woman could sense things about her that nobody else could.

"Nice to meet you, Sarah. And who's this?" She gestured to David, standing in the back.

"My brother, David."

"Hmmm. Does he need a crystal, too?"

"Um, well, I'm not exactly sure," Sarah said.

"Ah."

Sarah relaxed a bit when Cora turned her attention to Liam. "How's that school project going?"

He blushed and looked down at his feet.

"I think you better tell her, dude," Connor said.

"Er ... there really wasn't a project. At least, not a school one. I was seeing these weird visions when I touched an old record album of Connor's and I wanted to find out what it meant."

She watched him quietly as he told her about the album and the girl in the blue tie-dye shirt.

"Once we found Greg Ortman, everything fell into place, and I understood why she was bugging me." Liam looked around at his friends. "We did a good thing."

They all nodded.

"And we showed Sarah our crystals and told her about the energy and stuff," Molly said. "Now we're kinda working on another project, and Sarah needs to talk to you."

"Well." Cora said. "Crystals have amazing properties, and even though they work in subtle ways, the effects can be profound. What do you need help with, Sarah?"

Sarah glanced at Molly, who nodded. "Tell her."

Between Liam's psychic ability and Audrey's ghostly visits, she'd been in some strange situations, but somehow this seemed the oddest. *Should I really tell this stranger everything that's happening?* She looked around at her friends and remembered the stories they'd told about coming to see Cora. She wasn't a stranger, at least not to them, and she helped Liam ... a lot.

"It's the Orpheum. Mayor Scott is going to tear it down and build condos."

Cora made a face like she smelled something bad. "Well, well. I hadn't heard about that, but it doesn't surprise me overly much. That man is pretty interested in lining his own pockets."

"We want to get it designated as a historic site so they can't do it, but we're running out of time. We haven't found any real proof yet, and it seems like every time we come up with a plan or a next step, we just hit a wall."

Sarah paced to one of the shelves lined with crystals. The brightness of the stones registered in her awareness, but she didn't really see them. Instead, she saw the Orpheum screaming in pain as it collapsed into a pile of rubble. All of its beauty and the history contained within the walls gone forever. She dashed a tear away from her cheek and turned to Cora.

"Ozark is a special place, and I just wish I could get people to understand how important it is to preserve its history. Nobody's paying attention — well, except for my friends. My moms don't care. They're totally focused on themselves and making me and David move to Chicago. The mayor just wants to make money, and everyone else in town is oblivious." She walked back to stand with her friends. "So I guess what I need is for you to help me speak so that others really hear what I say. Is that even possible?"

Cora took both of Sarah's hands and gazed into her eyes. "There's something else, though, isn't there? Something deeper," she said gently.

Somehow, Sarah knew that Cora meant her mother, but her throat tightened so much she couldn't speak. Instead, she nodded and was relieved when Cora turned away.

"I definitely have something that can help you with that." Cora went to one of the shelves and grabbed a blue rock. "This is kyanite, and it's especially good for working with the Throat Chakra. Gives the ability to speak one's truth with clarity."

Could it be that simple? Sarah wondered. *A rock?*

"What the heck is a chakra?" Connor asked.

"It's an energy center in the body," Molly said.

"Very good, Molly." Cora smiled. "You're absolutely right."

"I've been reading up on crystals. Chakras are talked about a lot."

"*Chakra* is a Hindu word that means 'wheel of spinning energy,' and that's exactly what it is. Think of it as an invisible, rechargeable battery that's powered by the cosmos rather than electricity."

Cora walked over to a poster pinned to the wall. It showed the outline of a human body sitting cross-legged. Circles, the colors of the rainbow, were layered vertically from the base of the spine to the top of the head.

"This shows the locations on the body of the seven primary chakras." She pointed to the poster. "Come on. I'll show you what I mean."

She led them through a doorway and into another room. Brightly colored tapestries hung on the walls, and mats and cushions peppered the floor. In one corner was a narrow, padded, waist-high table. "Sarah, hop on up here and lie down on your back."

Not entirely sure of what she was getting into, Sarah glanced at Liam. When he nodded, she did as Cora asked and settled herself onto the table. It was surprisingly comfortable. Attached to the ceiling directly above was a picture of a beautiful forest landscape filled with fluttering butterflies. *Okay. This is weird.*

"So, the seven chakras are here." Cora pointed to the areas on Sarah's body. "You can't see them, but you can feel them. Molly, why don't you try first."

Molly moved to stand by the table.

"Remember during your last visit here, we talked about the energy field?"

"Sure. It's about this big and surrounds the whole body." She held her arms out.

"That's right. The chakras are a part of that field. They connect the energetic, or spiritual, body to the physical one." Cora held a hand out over Sarah's abdomen, palm down, and nodded. "Give me your hand," she said to Molly. She positioned Molly's hand in the same spot over Sarah's body, then stepped back. "What do you feel?"

Even though Molly's hand wasn't touching her, Sarah could feel the warmth of it. That wasn't surprising, but there was something else, a kind of tingly pressure—as if the hand was nested against her skin.

Molly stood perfectly still for a moment and then giggled. "It feels prickly on my palm."

"Now move your hand down to her leg. What do you feel?"

She placed her hand above her thigh. A moment passed, and Molly's brow furrowed. She looked at Cora. "Actually, I don't feel anything this time."

"Well, that's good. You shouldn't, because your hand isn't over one of the chakras. When your hand was over her abdomen, you were in contact with Sarah's solar plexus chakra. The energy is concentrated there, and you can feel it because the nerves in your palm are sensitive. There is no major chakra on her thigh, so you don't feel the energy."

"Wow!" Molly said. "That's really cool. I could actually feel it."

"You guys want to give it a try?" Cora asked.

Sarah was glad when Liam and Connor shook their heads, but David stepped forward eagerly. "I do." He held his palm out over Sarah's abdomen.

Sarah watched as David's face relaxed in concentration. Slowly, he moved his hand, hovering over each spot that Cora had pointed out. "It feels different here," he said to Cora, his hand over the hollow of Sarah's throat.

Almost immediately, Sarah felt the pressure intensify. The longer David's hand stayed on the spot, the more powerful it got. Her eyes filled with tears, and her throat tightened until she felt she was choking. No longer able to stand it, Sarah rolled to her side and coughed.

Cora patted her shoulder, until the coughing stopped. "You had quite a reaction," she said. "That area is where the throat chakra lies. Right now, yours is stuck. That's why you can't find the words to convey what you're feeling. If we can open it, you won't have that trouble anymore. Liam, would you go get that piece of kyanite I showed Sarah earlier? I think I set it on the counter."

When he came back with it, Cora said, "Hand it to Sarah."

He dropped it in her palm. The stone felt cool and seemed to pulse with pins and needles, almost like a very slight electric shock. Holding it was uncomfortable at first, but then the sensation shifted. It became warm and almost comforting. The tension in her throat eased. *Wow, that feels a ton better.* She gripped the stone tighter and started to sit up.

"No, no. Stay right there for another minute," Cora said. She gestured to David. "Try that spot again and see if it feels different to you."

He positioned his palm over Sarah's throat again. "Stronger."

"Good." Cora helped Sarah off the table. "That stone is the right one for you and will help you say what's in your heart."

"What just happened?" Connor asked Liam.

"I think Cora just taught us something else about energy, but I'm not exactly sure what."

This is amazing. Maybe there is something to all this energy and stones stuff. "I don't really know why, but my throat doesn't feel tight anymore," she said.

"That's wonderful, Sarah, but there's something more that I want to help you with." Cora took Sarah's hands again and Sarah felt the tingly warmth move up her arms. "Energy is a funny thing. Sometimes it gets stuck in, and on, us even when it's someone else's energy."

"That doesn't make any sense at all," Sarah said.

"I know, it's a strange idea. But every time we interact with others, energy is being exchanged. Have you ever felt fine and then had a fight with someone and felt a bit yucky afterward?"

"Sure. I don't like to fight with people. It makes my stomach hurt."

Cora smiled. "I'm sure you don't, but there's more to it than that. Besides harsh words, energy is also traded. You can think of it as little arrows shooting off the person. Those arrows can get stuck in your energy field. Most of the time, they just fall off, but sometimes they work their way deeper into the energy field. You have one of those deep arrows. It's from your mother. Can you tell me about her?"

"Not really." Sarah shot a look at her friends, startled by the change in direction. "She ... uh ... she abandoned me when I was three days old. I have no idea who she is or what happened to her."

"Ah, I see," Cora said. She briefly tightened her grip on Sarah's hands, then let go. "It's likely that part of the reason you can't speak up for yourself is because your mother couldn't either. I'm going to remove the energy now and I think you'll feel much better."

Cora made a motion like she was picking a piece of lint off Sarah's chest. She tossed it over her shoulder. "There. All gone. With what you're trying to accomplish, you'll need your voice." She turned away and walked back into the main store.

Sarah watched her go, then looked at her friends. "Whoa. What was that?"

"We told you she was a little woo-woo," Liam laughed.

"Yeah, but I never expected this," Sarah said.

"How do you feel?" Molly asked.

Sarah blew out a breath. "I'm not sure. Better, definitely better."

"Sorry about your mom, Sarah." Connor put a gentle hand on her back.

"Thanks. It's okay. I've gotten used to the idea that I'll never know her."

"Young man." Cora called, gesturing to David. "I think I have the perfect stone for you, too."

She went to the shelves and selected a shiny deep green stone with tiny flecks of red. She dropped it into his hand. After a moment, he nodded. "I can feel a slight vibration."

"That's a tumbled piece of bloodstone, also known as heliotrope. It comes from Africa and is actually starting to become rare. It's been used for thousands of years for its healing properties. It helps to overcome worry and will give you an energy boost when you need it."

"Thanks."

She patted his shoulder. "I'm glad you told me what's happening with the Orpheum, Sarah. I wish you luck with saving it. Trying to deal with Mayor Scott can be challenging."

"I hope we can find proof before it's too late," Sarah said.

"You know, back when I was just a little older than you, there were a lot of things going on that my friends and I didn't like. We tried to speak up about them, but it seemed like no one would listen to us, either."

"Really? What'd you do?"

"Well, we tried to bring awareness to the situation by protesting."

"Cool," Connor said. "Like back in the '60s. I've watched tons of documentaries about that. My folks love that stuff."

"Yes. We made signs and got people to gather in public places. We sang songs and shouted slogans. It's easy for the 'powers that be' to overlook a couple of kids. But if an entire town is making a racket, that's a lot harder to ignore."

"A protest," Sarah said. "Yeah. Maybe that would work." She started toward the door and turned back. "Cora, I have one more question. Do you think ghosts exist?"

"Absolutely. Einstein said 'Energy cannot be created or destroyed. It can only be changed from one form to another.' If everything is energy, including humans, then when we die, that energy doesn't die with the body. It has to be transformed in some way. I believe it goes into spirit form."

"Have you ever seen a ghost?" Sarah asked.

"Only once, and the experience has stayed with me always. Having an ability that gives you access to the spirit realm would be very special ... and quite a responsibility."

Sarah stared at Cora for a moment. *A responsibility?* She hadn't thought of that. Did the fact that she knew that the Orpheum was more than just an old building have something to do with why this was happening? *Did the Orpheum pick me to save it?* That idea made her more determined than ever.

"Thank you, Cora," Sarah said. She stepped out into the bright sunlight on the porch. "Come on, guys. I know what to do next."

"Yeah? What?" Liam asked.

"I think Mayor Scott's being sneaky about this. Cora's a downtown business owner, and she didn't know a major building was being torn down."

"Mr. Lewis didn't know about it, either," Molly said. "Probably nobody else does."

"Maybe he's trying to rush the demolition through before anyone can stop him," Connor said.

"That's what I think. We're going to let this whole town know what's going on, and maybe that will buy us enough time to search for the proof."

"Okay, but how?" Liam asked.

"By staging a protest. I'm going to chain myself to the door of the Orpheum." Sarah grinned. "They won't bulldoze it with a kid in the way."

"Cool," Connor said. "You're not doing it alone, though. I want to do it, too."

Liam ran a hand through his black hair. "Oh, man, I don't know. I just got first chair in orchestra. If I get in trouble again..."

"No worries," Sarah said. "This is my idea, and nobody has to do it with me."

"Well, I'm in," Molly said. "Liam, don't be such a dork. We're the Mud Street Misfits. We stick together."

Sarah stared at her friend, hoping he would join them, but understanding why he might not. It was a crazy idea, but she was doing it. Saving the Orpheum was her legacy to Ozark, and this might be the only way to make that happen.

"We are going to get into so much trouble for this." Liam grinned.

"Awesome, dude." Connor stuck his hand into the circle, and the others did the same. "The Orpheum," he said, and the others echoed it.

"Liam, Molly, Connor, go tell your folks you're spending the night at our house." Sarah rattled off instructions as they walked to their bikes. "David and I will take care of the chains we'll need. We also have poster board. Meet us at my house as soon as you can."

"What about Mrs. Miller?" Molly asked. "Isn't she staying with you while your moms are gone?"

"Don't worry about her. She's half deaf. You can stay in the basement, and she'll never know you're there."

As they pedaled away, Sarah shouted after them, "Bring some markers."

Liam waved a hand over his head, and they disappeared around the corner.

They biked toward home. David was quiet, as usual, and that was fine with her. *I'm going to get in so much trouble, but what could they do to me that would be worse than moving away? And if I save the Orpheum, it'll be worth it.* She finally had some direction, and it felt like they had a chance to stop the destruction of the beautiful building. "This is going to work, David. I just know it is," she said as they stepped onto their porch.

"Well, we better hurry," he warned, pointing over her shoulder.

She heard the rumble and spun around. A large truck towing a low-boy trailer slowly passed by. Sarah's heart sank when she saw the excavator hunkered on the back. She knew exactly where it was going. Their time was running out.

CHAPTER EIGHT

Sarah stood, hands on hips, surveying the cluttered cellar. "Where are those handcuffs? I hope Mom didn't send them to auction."

"Last time I saw them..." With a grunt, David hauled the irons out of the wooden crate and clanked them onto the concrete floor.

Sarah shuffled them around with the toe of her sneaker. "Three pair. That's perfect. Now we need a large padlock to attach us to the chain on the door."

David held out the one he'd already found. "Done."

The doorbell rang as they were coming up from the cellar. "I hope that's not Mrs. Miller," Sarah said and was relieved to see her friends standing on the porch.

She hurried them in and quickly shut the door. "You didn't leave your bikes out front, did you?"

"Duh! This is not our first rodeo," Connor said. "They're on the side of the house opposite Mrs. M's."

"Good." Sarah nodded. "We better get started. Gotta get the signs done before she gets here, and I'm not real sure when that'll be."

"I thought we'd need these." Connor held up four long, flat wooden strips. "They're paint stirrers that my dad had stashed. We can use them for sign posts."

They dumped the supplies on the family room floor and each grabbed a piece of poster board.

"What should we say?" Molly asked.

"Stuff like, *Save the Orpheum* or *Down with Demolition*," Connor said.

Molly scrunched up her face. "Down with demolition? That sounds lame."

"Well ... whatever. That's the best I could do on the spur of the moment. You think of something."

Everyone but Liam was finished when the doorbell rang, but markers, pieces of poster board, snack wrappers, and soda cans were strewn everywhere.

"Oh, no! She's here," Sarah said.

"Go let her in, but take your time. We'll get this taken care of," David said.

Before Sarah could get to the door, the bell rang again. "All right, all ready. I'm coming," she muttered and then smiled brightly at the older lady standing on the porch.

"Hi, Mrs. Miller." Sarah stepped out onto the porch and pretended to study the front yard.

"Are you looking for something?" Mrs. Miller asked.

"What? Oh, no. It's just such a lovely evening, isn't it?"

"Well, I suppose so, but can we go inside? I'd like to sit down. My bunions are killing me."

"Oh, uh, sure. Come on in."

Sarah stepped slowly through the door, careful to block the woman so that she had to follow behind her down the hall. "Sorry for the..." She trailed off when she found no evidence of what she and her friends had been up to.

"Hi, Mrs. M." David stepped through the basement door and shut it behind him. "Let me help you with that."

He took the cloth grocery bag and set it on the kitchen counter.

"So sorry to hear that you are moving away from Ozark," Mrs. Miller said. "You have been such wonderful neighbors. So quiet and unassuming."

"Uh ... thanks," Sarah said. "You didn't need to bring food. Our moms will be back tomorrow night."

"Oh, I know, dear. But they left in such a hurry, I wasn't sure what you'd have here. And I do like my chips and salsa with my shows."

* * *

Sarah came down the basement steps with plates of PB&J sandwiches for her guests. "I thought she'd never go to bed,"

"Will she check on you if she wakes up?" Molly asked.

"Nah," David said.

Sarah handed plates around, then sat on the rug and pulled one set of irons into her lap. "This is what we'll use to chain ourselves."

"Handcuffs? Like for prisoners?" Molly asked.

"Yup. These're from a territorial prison in Wyoming. 1800's era. Mom bought them at an auction. Once we lock ourselves into them, it'll take bolt cutters to get us out."

"Kinda creepy. The idea of people being in prison, I mean," Molly said.

"Yeah, I know what you mean. We've been to a few old places like that 'cause Mom-Heather loves the history that's there, but the places do feel really weird. That must be the energetic thing that Cora talks about."

"If these are antiques, aren't they kind of valuable?" Connor asked. "Your mom may not be too happy about them getting ruined."

"Yeah, I know. But it's not like we can go to the hardware store and buy chain."

"Having Mom mad because of the cuffs is the least of the problems with this plan," David said.

"What could possibly go wrong?" Sarah joked. Mentally ticking off a list of potential problems that made her heart thump. She kept it to herself, but the troubled look on her brother's face concerned her.

David paced across the room and back, then sat on the floor with her. "What would be the very worst thing that would happen if the Orpheum was lost?" he asked her.

"What? I thought you were on my side with this."

"I will always be on your side, Sarah. But this..." He pushed at the shackles, nodded to the pile of protest signs. "It's lowering to Scott's level. Kinda like what Brandon, Kaylee, and Dylan do."

"We're not bullying anyone," Sarah said.

"No, but it just seems wrong. It sends the wrong message."

"Wow. I... You've been talking about this? Do the rest of you feel the same way?"

"Kinda," Molly said.

"It's a cool idea. And I'd love to see the look on Mayor Scott's face when they find us," Connor said. "But it's sort of like using violence to prevent violence."

"We'll all get in trouble, but so what? We've been there before. It just seems that a protest takes away from the reason we want to save the Orpheum in the first place," Liam said.

"He's right. We want to save it because of its beauty and importance to the town. The people alive now should get to enjoy what people before did. But something like this will ... er ... taint the memory of it," David said.

Sarah looked around at her friends. Their eyes were sympathetic, but they nodded in agreement.

"But Mayor Scott will win," she whispered.

"Maybe ... yes. This time." David laid a gentle hand on her arm.

"If I don't save it, then all of the memories and cool things that happened there would be gone."

David shook his head. "Even if the Orpheum disappears, the memories will still be there. They live in the hearts and minds of the people who experienced them, not in the building. Will you forget the times we snuck in there? All the fun we had?"

"Of course not! But what Mayor Scott's trying to do is so wrong. He hasn't told anyone, and people have a right to know."

"That's true, and I don't like his methods, either. You know me, I'm all for fighting for what's right, but..." He picked up a set of the handcuffs and let them drop to the floor. "This is not the way."

Sarah bent her head. Tears slid down her cheeks and dropped onto the rusted iron, darkening it to burnished red. All that she'd worked for, the history that she wanted to preserve for this town, would be gone with one brutal bite of the dozer's jaws. When she was inside the theater, it was as if it lived—a heart throbbed, lungs breathed, the air shimmered with emotion. Destroying it would be like killing a living thing. *Just like in my dream.*

Clearly, she saw the vast auditorium. People gathered to see a musician or a group of actors, hoping to be taken away from the reality of their lives for a while. They coalesced into a miasma of clothing and hairstyles that changed over the generations. Some people laughed, some cried. It was a place where lives were impacted, changed, made better or worse. For her, it was like being surrounded by a huge family that had always been a part of her life.

But she'd done all she could. The solution wasn't going to drop out of the sky between now and Saturday.

"You're right. So much for my great idea, huh? I'll leave Ozark, and no one'll remember me." It felt as if she were shrinking, her body preparing to rise above the earth like a thistledown set free to sail the sky, to be forever at the mercy of circumstances she couldn't control.

"What? You're nuts. You're our friend, and you'll always be." Molly sat down beside her and took her hand. "We won't forget you ... ever."

Sarah leaned her forehead against Molly's. *This is what friendship is. I hope I'll find it again.*

Suddenly, the strong odor of cigarette smoke wafted over her.

"Do you smell something funny?" she said, looking around.

"It wasn't me," Connor said.

"Oh, Connor, not that. I smell cigarettes."

"Does Mrs. Miller smoke?" Liam asked.

Sarah stood up. "I think it's Audrey."

"She's here? Where?" Molly looked around. "I want to see her."

Sarah felt a gentle pressure on the top of her head and the whisper of breath across her cheek.

Sing for us. The raspy voice was a butterfly caress on her ear.

Could the memories of the Orpheum really be sustained without the building? Will my memories of Ozark and my wonderful friends go away just because I don't live here anymore? No! Absolutely not! She realized that just like her life here needed to be celebrated, so did the Orpheum's life. "Guys, you're not going to believe this, but I have another idea." She looked at her friends.

"Did you think of somewhere else we can look for proof?" Liam asked.

"Nope. Something better. David's right. Even if we were successful and the building did stay, if the stories aren't told, the memories will eventually fade. It's not just about saving the physical structure of the building—it's about preserving those memories. We need to find a way to do that. So, rather than fighting with the mayor, let's hold a celebration for the Orpheum.

"We bring people together to rejoice in what the Orpheum means to them and this town. Give them a way to share their memories and experiences. The Orpheum deserves a party to celebrate its life, not tears to mourn its death. Let's send it out with a bang."

"Yes!" Connor said. "A big honkin' party,"

"When?" Liam asked.

"Saturday, during the farmers' market?" Sarah said.

David smiled. "I like it."

"Let's do more posters—this time letting everyone know about the celebration. We can put them up around town," Molly suggested.

As she looked around at her friends, Sarah became grounded again. The drifting sensation left her and the substance of her body returned. The loss of the Orpheum was sad, but the memory of what it meant to the town would remain. Just like the memories of all that she'd had in Ozark would go with her and be a part of her new life in Chicago.

CHAPTER NINE

After school, the Misfits sat around the picnic table by the fountain, tossing out ideas for the Orpheum celebration. "We should have music!" Molly said.

"Definitely," Sarah said, remembering Audrey's voice in her ear. "But who can we get?"

"How about the school orchestra?" Liam said. "I bet Mr. Walsh would be into it!"

"Yeah, and that would mean that all of the parents would be there," Connor added.

"Good thinking." Sarah turned to Liam. "Could you perform an old Elvis song or something like that?"

Liam laughed. "That's not really our type of music."

"Why can't *we* do it?" Molly asked.

"You don't look like an Elvis impersonator to me," Connor said.

"No, and you don't either. But that doesn't mean that we can't sing an Elvis song."

"She's right," Sarah said. "Remember when we pretended to play that Elvis song the night we snuck into the Orpheum? It was as if the building really liked it."

"Yup." Molly nodded. "And it would be really happy if we did it for real. Connor, you play guitar. Liam plays the bass, and Sarah can sing. We're most of the way there."

"Oh, I'm not too crazy about singing in public," Sarah said.

"Get real. It's for the Orpheum." Connor nudged her. "And we'll be with you."

She imagined herself standing on a stage, all those eyes staring at her, waiting for her to mess up or look stupid. Just the thought of it made her throat tighten. Then she remembered the warmth that had surrounded her on the Orpheum stage. It came not just from her friends, but the building, too, and now she was sure, from the spirits that dwelt there. It was one of the reasons it had seemed so important to save it. Her fingers closed around the piece of kyanite in her pocket. "Okay. I'll do it."

"I can play the ukulele ... sort of." Molly smiled. "Now all we need is a drummer."

They all looked at David, who was tapping a rhythm on the table. "What?" he said and they laughed.

"Do you really think we can pull this off?" Sarah asked.

"I know we can," Liam said. "All we need to do is learn one song."

"There's not much time," David said.

"We have to start practicing right away," Molly said.

"And we have to get permission for the party. That means talking to Mayor Scott again."

"Sarah, you can't do that on your own," Liam said. "I'll go with you."

"We'll all go," David said. "Show of strength and solidarity."

"Nice." Connor nodded. "Sarah, you do the talking, and we've got your back."

"When?" Molly asked.

Sarah looked over at the city hall building. The clock in the tower said *4:45*. "We do it now."

"You sure?" Molly. "Like now, now?"

"May as well get it over with," Liam said.

Connor said, "Heck yeah, let's do it!"

They stood and instinctively gathered into a circle. The image of the swirling chakra energy that Cora described came into Sarah's mind. That was what they did for each other—provided the strength to do what needed to be done.

"No matter what happens, we're in this together," Sarah said.

"Mud Street Misfits to the end," Connor said, and stuck his hand into the center of the circle.

They echoed the cheer, then turned toward City Hall and, like a precision marching band, crossed the street and tramped up the marble steps.

***

Sarah stepped up to the receptionist. "We'd like to talk with Mayor Scott, please."

The woman gave them a cool-eyed stare. "And what is your business with the mayor?"

"My name is Sarah Barrett, and these are my friends. We're here to talk to the mayor about the Orpheum." Sarah tried to speak in her best adult voice, but she could feel tightness creeping into her throat.

"Mayor Scott is a very busy man. It would be best if you made an appointment for, say..." She flipped pages on a small calendar by her phone. "Two weeks from now."

What? No way! I'm not going to be pushed around anymore. Sarah fiercely clasped the piece of kyanite in her pocket and slapped her hand on top of the calendar. "We can't wait two weeks, er..."—she glanced down at the name plaque on the woman's desk— "Ms. Marshall. We need to see him now. It's about a celebration, a ... a rally."

"Music and dancing. A party," Connor added. "You know ... fun."

The receptionist eyed them suspiciously, but she picked up the phone. "Have a seat, and I'll see if he can make time for you."

They sat silently on uncomfortable chairs in the drab waiting room. Connor flipped through an *ESPN Magazine*, and with each turned page, Sarah wanted to grab it out of his hands, rip it into a gazillion pieces, throw them on the ground, and stomp on them. How could he stay so relaxed, no matter where he was or what went on around him? Then Cora's voice came into her head. "Just breathe. It will all be fine." *I can do this. I can do this*, she repeated to herself.

The phone on the receptionist's desk buzzed, and Sarah jumped.

"Mayor Scott will see you now," Ms. Marshall said. Her high heels clicked as she walked to a large door across the room. She hesitated a moment, eyeing them. "He expects perfect behavior."

Sarah took a deep breath and walked into the office. The others followed.

Mayor Scott's large wooden desk sat atop a slight platform in the corner of the room. It wasn't as high as a stage, just a few inches, but it raised him enough so that he appeared bigger than he was. It made Sarah think of the Wizard in Oz, and the silliness helped her relax a bit.

Mayor Scott looked at them, his lips pursed. He waved the assistant away and with the click of the door behind her, the room seemed to shrink. The air was sticky and had a stale odor that reminded Sarah of the gym locker room. The pudgy man sat back in his chair and folded his hands over his belly.

"Well, what do you want?"

Sarah swallowed around the lump in her throat and tightened her grip on the stone in her pocket. "Mayor Scott, I know you know that we were trying everything we could to keep the Orpheum from being torn down." The mayor said nothing, so Sarah rushed on. "But we understand now that we can't save it."

"That's true. It's scheduled for demolition this Saturday."

"Saturday!" Sarah gasped. "We thought ... never mind. It doesn't matter now. What we would like to ask is if we could put on a celebration for the Orpheum before it's gone. A party where people can listen to music, have some food, and tell their stories of the building. Talk about their experiences. We'll do all the work, and there won't be any cost. It'll be a potluck."

Mayor Scott sat forward and put his hands on his desk. "When would you hold this celebration?"

"Saturday, during the farmers' market," Liam said.

"Right before the wreckers do their job." Mayor Scott smiled.

Oh, yuck, Sarah thought and shivered. *Almost done. Almost done.*

"Okay," Mayor Scott said. "I'll let you have your little party, and then we'll end it with a bang as we bring the building down. That will really show the people that progress is what we're all about."

Sarah thought that was a horrible idea, but at least they would get their chance. "So we have your okay?"

He slapped the top of his desk, pushed his chair back, and stood up. "Sure, sure. Go ahead. But start early, because that building is coming down at noon. Sharp!" He turned and looked out the window, then back at them. "I thought you kids were going to be trouble, but looks like you were actually helpful ... this time. Now run along. I have important things to do."

***

Sarah slid onto the bench at the picnic table and took a gulp of fresh air.

"I don't know if I feel good or bad about what just happened in there," Molly said.

"I know the feeling. That man is disgusting."

"Yeah, but at least we get to have our party," Connor said.

"There's not much time to get this together. It seems pretty overwhelming," Molly said.

"But we can do it. We have to do it. The Orpheum is counting on us. I'll create a flyer tonight, and me and David will put it up around town."

"I'll talk to Mr. Walsh about getting some of the orchestra to play on Saturday. It's short notice, so I don't think we can get everyone, but we'll get some."

"Do you really think we can pull off an Elvis song by Saturday?" Sarah asked.

"Of course, we can," Connor said. "That's going to be the coolest thing about all of this.

We get to be rock stars for a day. I'll find a great song for us."

"Hey," Molly said, pointing across the street to the Orpheum. "Isn't that Mayor Scott?"

"Yeah, he's going into the Orpheum," Connor said.

Sarah gasped, pulled Molly's arm down, and slugged Connor on the shoulder.

"Ouch. What'd you do that for?"

"Don't look over there. We don't want to draw any attention to ourselves. What if he changes his mind and won't let us have the celebration?"

"Why do you think he's going in there?" Molly asked, sneaking a peek over her shoulder.

"Probably wants to gloat over what he's destroying," Liam said.

"He's got a key. That's interesting. Do you suppose it was him in there the night we stayed?" Sarah asked.

"Oh, that's even creepier than zombies." Molly shivered.

"Well, whatever it is, let's get out of here before he comes out," Sarah said. "I don't think I can take getting slimed by him again."

As they left the park, Sarah looked back over her shoulder at the building. The chain hung askew on the front door, and she swore there was a flash of light at the window. *I wonder what he's up to in there? Was he the person they saw the night they were in the Orpheum? If so, who was the person with him?*

***

Heather and Rachel appeared in the doorway of Sarah's bedroom. "You two have been in here all evening. What's up?"

"Oh, nothing," Sarah said, closing the laptop cover.

Rachel walked over and held out her hand. "Let me see."

Sarah handed her the device and shot an 'uh oh' look at her brother.

"It's nothing, really. We're doing a celebration for the Orpheum this Saturday. David and I are creating a flyer to put up around town."

Rachel accessed the file they'd been working on and showed it to Heather.

"A Celebration of the Orpheum," Heather read. "So you've given up on getting the certification?"

Sarah nodded and felt her throat beginning to close up.

"We tried to find the proof that we needed," David said. "But ..." he shrugged.

"Well, I'm really proud of you guys," Heather said.

"You are?" Startled, Sarah looked at her mom. "Why?"

"Because you recognized a futile effort when you saw it," Rachel said.

Heather placed a hand on Rachel's arm. "No, I'm proud because you tried. You went after something you wanted and even though you didn't get it, I'm sure you learned a lot in the process."

Did I learn something, Sarah wondered? She thought back over the rollercoaster ride of their attempt to save the Orpheum. She thought of Steve Lewis, and Cora, and even Ms. Blue who had been sad about the Orpheum being destroyed. The tightness in her throat eased.

"I learned that there are places in the world that are special and people who are kind and caring. That just because I was abandoned once, that doesn't mean it will ever happen again. And, I learned that my friends, family, and home are the most important things in my life.

"I know now that there're things in life that I don't have any control over; like the Orpheum being destroyed and leaving my friends and this town I love. That really sucks, but ... it's just the way it is."

"Now we need to get this flyer out to as many people as possible so that we have a huge crowd at the celebration on Saturday," David said.

"Well, we can help you with that," Heather said. "Email it to both of us. I'll send it to my Friends of the Museum list. Just the sort of people who would show up for an event like this. I'm sure Rachel has some folks already in mind that she would send it to, right?"

Heather looked at Rachel and one of those unsaid messages passed between them. "Sure," Rachel said. "Of course."

"That would be awesome," Sarah said. "Thanks."

"How are you getting the music," Heather asked.

"Liam's talking to Mr. Walsh to see if we can get the school orchestra to play and we're going to do a song, too."

"We?" Rachel asked.

"The Mud Street Misfits. I'm going to sing, and David's playing the drums. Liam on bass, of course. Connor on lead guitar – of course, again, and Molly plays the ukulele."

"Wow! Our Sarah singing in public and David on the drums," Heather said. "I'm sure it will be great"

Their moms kissed them both and Rachel ruffled David's hair. "Don't stay up too late, you two."

"That was a little weird," David said, once their moms were gone.

"No kidding. I wonder what they're up to now?" Sarah said.

CHAPTER TEN

The lunch room rumbled with voices as students rushed in to grab food. Sarah could barely hear Liam over the clatter of trays. "I talked to Mr. Walsh this morning. He said he'll do it. It won't be a mandatory performance, but he still thinks a lot of the kids will show up."

"It's a good thing, since Sarah put it on the flyer," Connor said.

"I knew that Liam would make it happen," Sarah said.

"He asked about chairs and stands, which we don't have, but hopefully whoever participates can bring their own. He suggested the Chopin piece we've been working on."

Connor wrinkled his nose. "Uh, dude, I don't think Chopin and Elvis go together."

"Yeah, I know. I told him that something lighter would be better. Maybe like the Leroy Anderson medley. It has a great jazz feel to it. We've only just started to learn it, but I think the group can pull it together."

"Jazz? Good idea. That will get the people all *jazzed* up for the celebration." Connor did a seat-boogie.

"I got a text from my mom a few minutes ago. She sent the flyer to the Friends of the Museum list. I also sent it to Steve Lewis. He probably has a ton of contacts, since he's a writer. You guys have a digital copy. See if your folks will send it to their friends. Connor, have you come up with a song?" she asked.

"Yup. 'Jailhouse Rock.' It's not too hard so I think we can do it." He played it quietly on his phone.

Sarah closed her eyes and listened, imagining them performing and the Orpheum listening. She smiled. "It's perfect."

"My folks said we can use the garage to practice," Connor said. "They won't be there until later tonight, but come over at 7:00. Don't forget your instruments."

"When I told my dad about performing the song, he got kind of excited," Liam said. "He's got a ton of mics and amps and even an old drum set that David can use. I have no idea why he has all that stuff, but I think he was happy that he'd finally get to use it for something. We'll bring it all over."

"Gotta get to algebra," Connor said. "I'll see you rock stars tonight." He high fived them both, then merged into the crowd of students.

"I've never sung over a microphone." Sarah looked at Liam. "It'll be hard enough standing on the stage, but with my voice amplified..."

"I get that." Liam nodded. "But you have a really awesome voice, Sarah. People will love it. Just keep the stone Cora gave you close by."

"I guess," Sarah said, not entirely sure this was a good idea after all.

"It's for the Orpheum," Liam reminded her.

"You know what, you're absolutely right. It's for the Orpheum." *And it's the least I can do for it.*

***

When Sarah and David walked into Connor's garage that night, it looked like a music equipment bomb had gone off. Cords, amps, and instruments were scattered everywhere. Liam and his dad were setting up the drum kit.

"That should do it," Lloyd said as they stepped back.

"You ready to rock, Ringo?" Connor slung his arm around David's shoulders.

David didn't answer, just stared at the drums, looking a little sick. Sarah knew that he was as worried about playing the drums as she was about singing. She started to go over to him, then stopped when Liam's dad grabbed a pair of sticks and sat down behind the drums. He was a bear-sized man but he had a gentle way about him. He seemed to sense that David was nervous and calmly filled the room with a beat.

David won't be able to resist that for long, Sarah thought, and gradually, David edged closer. Pretty soon, Lloyd was telling him about the individual drums that made up the set and showing David some techniques.

"The nice thing about drumming," Lloyd told David, "is that there are no notes. You just have to have rhythm. You have that, right?"

"I think so."

"I think so, too." Lloyd clasped a hand on the boy's shoulder and then handed him the drumsticks.

When David slid confidently onto the leather seat, Sarah relaxed. *Now, if I can get comfortable singing in public, it will all come together.*

"This is so cool," Connor said. "We have everything we need. I always wanted to be in a garage band." He grabbed the sheets of music he'd prepared, put a copy on each stand, then slipped his guitar strap over his head. He turned some knobs on the amp and riffed a couple of notes. The sound filled the garage.

Liam walked to a microphone on a stand. "Sarah, this is your mic. There's an on-off switch here, and the sound will run through that amp." He turned the equipment on. "Test one, two." His voice careened off the walls in a high-pitched squeal. He fiddled with the controls on the amp, then stepped back. "That should do it."

"Molly, since your uke doesn't have a pickup, we set you up with this mic. Play right in front of it, and it'll come out that amp."

Molly nodded and unzipped her bag to get the ukulele out.

Liam walked back to his spot and settled the bass strap on his shoulders. "David, you don't need an amp. Those drums are loud enough."

He did a thumbs up and crashed the cymbals.

"Okay, Connor. Now what?"

"Uh, what do you mean?"

Sarah smiled at the stunned look on his face. "You picked the song, prepared the music, and it's your garage. It makes sense that you should direct us, too."

"Well, uh … okay. You all have the music sheet on your stand. It shows the chords and lyrics." He pulled out his phone and hooked it up to an amp. "Let's give the song a listen and then try to play it."

When the music started, a fluffy golden head popped up over the edge of the wooden pen in the corner and howled. They all burst out laughing.

Molly hurried over and picked up the pup. "Oh, my goodness. You've grown so much. Dad, this is the one that I told you about. Isn't he beautiful? Can we have him?"

"Molly…" Lloyd frowned. "I told you…"

"Dad, please. I will do everything for him. You won't even know he's there."

Lloyd rubbed one of the pup's paws and shook his head. "I don't think that's even possible. Look at the size of these feet! He's going to be a big boy."

Molly clutched the puppy tighter. "Will you at least think about it? He's so sweet and he's all alone. I know you would love him. Mr. Harrison already said it was okay."

"Yeah, well, I'll need to talk to him about that." Lloyd ran a hand through his short hair and sighed. "I'll think about it, and I need to talk to Jennifer. Put him down and get back to practice."

Molly set the pup on the floor and rubbed his head. When Connor started "Jailhouse Rock" on his phone, the pup howled again and then began walking around the garage, wagging his tail and wiggling his butt.

"Look, he's dancing." Molly laughed.

"You know who he reminds me of?" Connor asked.

"Yup." Liam said. "Elvis."

"Oh, Dad. Now we have to get him." Molly pleaded. "I'll name him Elvis, and he can be the Mud Street Misfits' mascot."

As Lloyd watched the puppy, the edges of his mouth twitched as if he wanted to laugh. Sarah felt pretty sure that the pup would be going home with Molly and Liam.

***

They listened to the song three times, and then Connor said, "Okay. Let's give it a try."

He counted them off, and they began to play. When quiet descended, they looked at each other and started laughing.

"Wow, that was really bad!" Molly said.

"Oh, man! We have a long way to go," Connor agreed.

"You know," Liam said, "considering that was the first time playing together, it wasn't that bad."

"Yes, it was," Sarah said with a wry look.

"Rome wasn't built in a day," Connor said.

"Yeah, but they had more than four days to build it. That's all we have," David reminded them.

"We can do it," Liam said. "We need to play and listen to each other. That's what makes good groups great."

"Let's try it again, but this time, play along with the recording," Connor suggested.

Sarah wasn't sure how many times they played the song, but she could tell they were getting better. When she saw David yawn, she said, "I think that's enough for tonight. We'll get it. I know we will."

But as she turned off her mic, she wasn't so sure. The whole idea was to bring everyone together in celebration of the Orpheum but what if nobody showed up? The Orpheum was important to her but was it important to the town? Did they see it the way she did? She wouldn't know until Saturday.

***

Saturday morning, it was hard to ignore the activity around the Orpheum. Construction workers in yellow vests and hard hats were moving machinery into place and going over lists. Tears filled Sarah's eyes, but she blinked them back. *We're here to celebrate, not mourn.*

"The setup went fast. We still have almost an hour before people arrive," Liam said.

"Do you think they'd let us go in if we told them we wanted to look around?" Sarah asked, gesturing to two workers standing by the door.

"Maybe," Liam said. "It couldn't hurt to ask."

"That would be awesome," Connor said. "Though it'd feel a little weird, going in the front door."

Sarah called to David and Molly and motioned for them to follow.

"Excuse me," Sarah said. "We're the group that organized the Orpheum celebration for this morning. Do you think we could go in? Just for a few minutes."

The man holding the clipboard glanced at the other one standing with him.

"I don't see why not," he said. "The building hasn't been condemned. Head on in, but only for a few minutes, and be careful."

Connor pushed through the door, and the others followed him into the cavernous lobby.

"I just wish there was something more we could do." Sarah sighed.

Molly gave her a hug as the others huddled around.

"You know, maybe there is," Liam said. "All this time we've been looking for a way to save the Orpheum, but maybe that's not the right way to go about this. Remember when Cora told us that energy lives in every place and thing? Maybe there's some energy here that can help us. Energy that would help the Orpheum save itself."

"Dude." Connor shook his head. "I'm not even sure what that means."

"No. He's right," Sarah said, excitement shooting through her. "I can't believe I didn't think of it myself. I saw Audrey with my own eyes. We felt her in the control room. Maybe she can help us. Let's go sit on the stage. That's the heart of this building. If we listen, maybe the Orpheum or Audrey will tell us what to do."

Connor held the door open as they walked into the auditorium. Sarah glanced over at the rows and rows of seats and remembered when they were here before. Then, she'd felt as if the seats were full of people and that every eye was on her, hopeful of her success. *Please, please let this work.* She crossed her fingers as she climbed the steps to the stage.

She led them to center stage and they sat in a circle.

"Does everyone have their crystal with them?"

They pulled out the crystals that Cora had given them.

"Awesome." She grinned.

Sarah set hers in the center of their circle, and the others did the same. "Uh, okay. I feel a little silly doing this."

"Don't," Connor said. "Just do it. We don't have much time left."

She nodded and looked out at the vacant seats. "We really, really want to help you, but we don't know how. If you don't want to be torn down, please send us some kind of message. Something that will help us save you."

She looked back at her friends. "Now, I guess we relax and listen."

Sarah closed her eyes. At first, all she could hear was the annoying beeps from the big rigs out front and crew members shouting to each other. Eventually, as the quiet stillness of the building blanketed her, she heard the gentle breathing of her friends and the creaks and groans of the old wood. She thought of all the amazing things she'd experienced in this building.

It had been a roller coaster ride of excitement and despair as they'd tried to come up with a way to save it. *I've done everything I can, and now it's up to you to save yourself. If such a thing is possible, now is the time.* She thought briefly of the costumes they'd found. If she told the foreman, could they at least salvage them? As she formulated a plan, a ringing noise intruded into her thoughts. She opened her eyes to find the others staring at her.

"Do you hear that, or is it just me?"

"It's coming from backstage," Connor said.

"It's a phone," Molly said. "With an old-fashioned ring. I know because Janey's mom's cell has a ring like that."

"Somebody must've dropped theirs," Liam said.

"Probably one of the workers. We should go find it for them."

Sarah walked toward the edge of the curtain, following the sound. She heard the others behind her but felt separated from them. It was as if she were being pulled toward the ringing sound by a thread attached to her belly. The sensation was strange but not scary.

"Liam, would you activate your flashlight app?" Sarah asked. "It's dark back here."

Light flicked on and played into the recesses. She spotted a door and tried the knob. It protested but finally gave in. Inside, the room was inky-black, but the ringing was louder. Sarah took a cautious step forward and then another.

Molly's shriek tore through the air.

"What? What?" Sarah gasped.

"Didn't you see it? There're people in here. Zombies! I saw them."

"Hello," Liam said, stepping forward. "Is anyone in here?"

The beam of Liam's cell phone flashlight broke the darkness apart and bounded around the room. Sarah shrank back when the light illuminated faces.

"Who are you?" She demanded.

Only silence answered her.

"Let's get out of here," Connor said.

"Wait," David said. "Hand me the phone, Liam."

David shone the light directly opposite them and moved it from face to face.

"It's us," Sarah said. "A mirror."

"Oh, wow," Molly said, rubbing her chest. "I think I need to sit down. That was really scary."

"Nah. I wasn't scared," Connor said. "I knew that whoever it was, we could take them."

"Yeah, right," Sarah said. "That phone is not going to stop ringing. We have to find it."

"Guys, look." David shone the light on a counter that ran along the opposite wall under the mirror. It spotlighted the phone then bobbed along, tracing the cord that snaked out. It stopped at the frayed end that was clearly not plugged into anything.

"Is that the phone we found in the trunk?"

"No way," Liam said. "We left that in the office. How'd it get down here?"

"And how is it ringing?" Molly said.

"Must be long-distance," David said.

"Good one, dude." Connor grinned. "Who's going to answer it?"

Without looking at her friends, Sarah knew their eyes were on her. *Time for a phone conversation with a ghost.* She reached out, hesitated briefly, then snatched up the receiver. "Hello?" Static bubbled in her ear and then receded.

A scratchy but familiar voice garbled, "itss ... in ... kit."

The static rose again, but Sarah thought she heard her name spoken before the phone went dead. She set the handset back onto the cradle. "Okay. That was definitely one of the weirdest things that's ever happened to me."

"Tell us," Molly said. "Was someone there?"

"It was a woman's voice. I'm pretty sure it was Audrey. She said something that sounded like, 'It's in the skit.'"

"What? That's crazy," Liam said.

"Not any crazier than everything else that's happened."

"And we did ask the Orpheum for help," David pointed out.

"Oh my gosh," Molly breathed. "Sarah, you just talked to a ghost ... again. But what does it mean? The skit? Like a play?"

Sarah shrugged. "I have no idea. There haven't been any plays in the Orpheum in years."

She led them back to the stage and stood for a moment. "Audrey, I want to do what you're asking, but I don't understand." She gazed out across the auditorium and listened to the silence. "This is awful. We're so close, I can feel it. I just... I can't think of anything else. What about you guys? Liam, are you getting any visions?"

He shook his head.

Sarah's hand brushed the railing as she descended the steps. It seemed to vibrate warmly against her fingers. *It's in the skit. Skit? Audrey, I don't understand – what skit?* Out of the corner of her eye, Sarah saw a shimmer of silver lights that faded quickly away.

"Did you see that?" She walked over in front of the stage where the lights had hovered. A low railing separated the recessed area where the orchestra would have played during an opera or even a ballet. A few wooden chairs remained, strewn around on the once elaborately carpeted floor. "Pit," she whispered. "Not skit."

"Here. It's here." She shouted, whipping around to wave her friends over. "The orchestra *pit*. Quick, put on your lights."

"Look. There." Connor pointed to a small door with a heavy iron hasp, secured by a shiny new padlock.

Liam grasped it and tugged, but it stayed solidly locked.

"That's just great," Sarah said. "We get this far and need a hacksaw. Anybody got one of those?"

"No," David said. "But I have something that might help." He reached into his jeans pocket and pulled out a brass key.

"Where'd you get that?" Sarah asked.

"I found it in the desk drawer upstairs. It seemed out of place because it was so new. So I just..." He shrugged, and Sarah wanted to hug him.

"Do you think it'll fit?" Molly asked.

"Won't know till we try," Liam said. "You do the honors, David."

Sarah held her breath as her brother leaned forward to slide the key into the lock. It went in smoothly, and the padlock opened with a twist.

"All right." Connor slapped David on the back. "Nicely done, little dude."

Liam zipped the lock and key into his backpack. They stepped back as Sarah opened the door and then Liam shone his cell phone light into the black hole.

"I bet there're spiders in there," Molly said.

"Yup," Connor said. "Think I'll stay here and guard the door."

"Oh, stop being such a baby," Sarah said. "We're in this together, so we're all going ...

"What're we looking for?" Molly asked.

"I don't know. Anything that looks like it might help the Orpheum, I guess."

The doorway was low enough that they all had to bend over to clear the top of the jamb. Their cell phone torches revealed a closet-sized room stacked floor-to-ceiling with boxes.

"Look at all this stuff."

Connor opened the top of the box closest to him, reached inside, and brought out a rolled tube. He unfurled it and grinned, turning it around to show the others.

Sarah gasped.

The Orpheum's name was blazoned across the top of the poster, and below it read, *Tuesday July 6, The Famous Duke Ellington and his Orchestra. Dancing 9 to 1 a.m.*

"How's that for proof?" Connor asked Sarah.

"It's … amazing," she said, laughing.

Connor eased the top box off the stack so they could all look inside. They pulled out more posters, one after one, all showing famous people who'd performed at the Orpheum.

"Hey, Sarah, look at this one." David turned the poster around. *Sunday, February 6, 1953— In person at the Orpheum Auditorium, Elvis Presley and Johnny Cash.*

"I can't believe it! Audrey was right," Sarah said. Gently, she took the poster in her hands.

Connor set another box in front of her then moved further into the recesses of the small room.

"Oh, wow. Look at this." Inside were hundreds of photos. She grabbed a handful and shuffled through the images. "This is going to change everything. Thank you, Audrey! Thank you."

"Hey, guys," Connor called. "There's another door back here. It's got a lock on it, too, but it's really old. What do you suppose is in there?"

Anxiety hit Sarah like the percussion of a silent bomb blast. "No! Don't touch that," she cried. She grabbed Connor's arm just as he reached for the latch.

"Geez, chill," he said. "I wasn't going to hurt it."

Sarah stepped back, took a deep breath and the fear flowed away. "Uh, sorry. I just... it doesn't matter right now anyway," she said. "We've gotta show these things to the mayor. We can still stop the bulldozers. Come on."

CHAPTER ELEVEN

Each armed with pieces of Orpheum history, the Misfits ran out the front door of the Orpheum and right into Mayor Scott. He stumbled forward and into one of the councilmen, who just barely kept him from falling. "You! What are you doing here? Can't you see I'm giving a speech?"

"Wow, look at all these people," Liam exclaimed.

"Oh, it's wonderful. They all love the Orpheum, and we just found the proof we need to save it." Sarah beamed a smile out to the crowd.

"What are you talking about? There is no proof." Mayor Scott dismissed them and turned back to his audience.

"I've got it right here." Sarah held out the rolled-up poster of Elvis.

The mayor knocked the tube out of her hand. It skittered down the concrete steps and landed at the feet of a small, neatly dressed woman Sarah had only seen in photographs.

Mayor Scott groaned and ran down the few steps to the woman. The Misfits hurried after him.

"Why, Governor Lewis, so good of you to come to our little celebration of this marvelous old building," the mayor said. He nudged the tube away with his toe.

"My brother, Steve, told me about the demolition of the building and the rally. I thought I would come by and see for myself. My grandmother was very fond of this ding,"

Just then, Steve Lewis walked up and gave rah a wink.

"Governor Lewis is your *sister*?" Sarah asked.

"Yeah," he smiled sheepishly. "I must've forgotten to mention that."

The governor bent down to retrieve the rolled poster. Slowly, she unfurled it and read the contents. A gasp from the crowd made Sarah smile.

"I thought you said there was nothing that ties the Orpheum to any significant historical events?" she asked Mayor Scott.

"Uh ... er ... there is no proof. It was all destroyed."

She turned the poster around.

"Ah, well. Trinkets. Just because these nosy kids found some ... some ... souvenirs, does not mean anything. Progress! That's the important thing for this city."

"What!" Sarah said. "These aren't trinkets. Show them."

They all unfurled their posters and held them up so everyone could see.

"There's one about Duke Ellington and his orchestra," someone from the crowd exclaimed.

"Ella Fitzgerald and Louis Armstrong, too. That's amazing," a woman said.

"Even Hank Williams. Gosh, I would have loved to see that!"

The crowd rumbled, and Sarah had to raise her voice to be heard. "That's right. These are important pieces of Ozark history. This proves the Orpheum is more than just bricks. It's part of what makes this town great, and tearing it down is wrong."

Mayor Scott sputtered.

"Where did you get these?" Governor Lewis asked.

"In a small room behind the orchestra pit. There's a ton of stuff like this," Connor said.

"But maybe the mayor already knows that." Sarah held out her hand, and Liam pulled the shiny padlock out of his backpack. She showed it to the governor and then turned to Mayor Scott.

"Did you put the boxes in there, hoping they'd never be found?"

"Oh, that's ridiculous. This does not change anything. Progress will not stop because of a couple of old photos. If you insist, we can put these things in the museum, but the building must come down."

Governor Lewis looked from the lock to the poster and back to Mayor Scott. "Mr. Mayor, this is compelling evidence in favor of designating the Orpheum a historic site. Direct the demolition crew to stand down until all of the evidence can be removed from the building and documented."

"But I have all of the equipment ready to go. We can't just stop everything because of some silly posters."

Sarah sorted through the photos in her hand and handed one to the governor. She smiled, her hand sliding lightly over the image of her grandmother and her friends on stage, singing with Elvis.

"As governor of this state, I can tell you, Mayor Scott, that this building will be here for a very long time."

The crowd cheered.

Liam touched Sarah's shoulder. "You did it."

She opened her arms and brought the others into a group hug. "*We* did it." She thrust her hand into the center of their circle, and each one layered their hand on top. "Misfits to the end," she said, and she made no effort to stop the tears that slid down her cheeks.

"Let's party," Connor yelled.

***

It seemed that the whole town agreed with Connor, because there weren't enough tables to hold all the food that everyone had brought to share. Neighbors rushed to get more. Mr. Walsh set up his grill, and soon the parents were serving up hot dogs and hamburgers.

The orchestra set up close to the front steps of the Orpheum. They played the jazz numbers they'd been practicing and then launched into a medley of Louis Armstrong songs.

Sarah, Molly, David, and Connor stood together listening and watching Liam play his bass. It was a wonderful day. They'd saved the Orpheum, and that was the best thing ever, but a little niggle of fear set in when Sarah thought about being on stage in front of all these people. She knew the song. Goodness knows she'd practiced it enough. And it seemed especially appropriate to do the Elvis song after what they found in the boxes, but the thought of everyone listening to her voice still freaked her out.

She almost screamed when a hand touched her shoulder. "What an amazing thing you kids did," said a familiar voice.

She turned to find the two Greg Ortmans grinning at her. She hugged them both. The older Mr. Ortman took her hand. "You did a special thing, Sarah. I'm sure Elaine is smiling down on us right now."

"You know, I'm sure she is, too." Sarah hugged him again.

"You guys ready to rock and roll?" Liam asked, joining the group.

"Um ... I guess," Sarah said.

"Ah, come on, Sarah," Connor said. "If David can do it, so can you."

"For the Orpheum," the others said in unison.

The group walked to where Liam's dad had arranged the amps, mics, and music stands. The crowd quieted when they picked up their instruments. *I feel sick. I can't remember any of the words, and I'm going to spew all over the front row.*

With a hand pressed to her tummy, Sarah looked out across the sea of eyes. Her moms stood arm in arm in the front row, flanked by Liam, Molly, and Connor's folks. The Ortmans grinned at her. Steve and his sister stood to the side.

She spotted the familiar face of Cora a few rows back and wiggled her fingers in a wave.

Cora tapped her throat, smiled, and nodded. *My crystal.* Sarah closed her hand around it like a lifeline. She drew it out and set it on the music stand. *Here goes nothing.* With a quick breath, she flipped on her mic. "We're the Mud Street Misfits, and this song is for Audrey Lewis and the Orpheum."

Sarah performed the song perfectly. She forgot about the crowd and sang out her joy in the accomplishment of saving the Orpheum. *I'll still lose a lot of what I love, but I'll leave Ozark with an amazing history. That's enough.*

✻✻✻

Everyone gathered around when they finished the song.

"You kids really did pull it off," Steve Lewis said. "And that photo of Grandma is wonderful. Thank you for finding it."

"We couldn't have done it without you and your sister," Sarah said.

"And your grandmother's ghost," Connor muttered.

Sarah elbowed him in the side, and he whooshed out a breath of air.

"What?" Steve wrinkled his brow.

"Oh, don't pay any attention to him," Sarah said.

"So now what?" Steve asked Heather. "Will the Orpheum become a historic site?"

"First, we need to move the artifacts over to the museum and catalog everything. Once that's done, I'll prepare the paperwork and submit it to the committee. Considering we seem to have the governor on our side, I don't think getting the designation will be a problem," Sarah's mom explained.

"That's great. The Orpheum sure deserves to be preserved," he said.

"Except you won't be here to do it, Mom. Remember? We're moving to Chicago," Sarah reminded her.

"Oh, well. That's something we want to talk to you about, right Rachel?" Heather said.

Mom-Rachel went to Sarah and tipped her chin up to look her in the eye. "Honey, I am so sorry for all that I've put you through. Heather ... and you and David have made me see what an amazing place this is and how much it means to you." She held one hand out to Heather and the other to David. "So ... I talked to the senior partner at the firm here, and they're going to consider me for partnership this summer."

Sarah gaped at her mom. "What? We're not leaving?"

Heather and Rachel shook their heads. Sarah threw her arms around them, dragging David into the group hug. "Thank you! Thank you!"

The Misfits were hooting and hollering behind them, Connor high fiving everyone within reach.

"Yes, well, there is one other thing that needs to be solved," Heather said once everyone calmed down. "If we can't get someone to lease the building, the mayor may still be able to tear it down."

"What?" Liam turned to her. "Nobody ever said anything about that."

"That really stinks," Connor said.

"No! We can't lose it after all this," Sarah cried. "But who's going to want it in this shape?"

"I'll rent it." A voice from the back said. Everyone turned to find Lloyd standing close, his arms full of equipment. "I've always wanted to open a music store, maybe a place where musicians can perform. I could finally get some use out of all this stuff I have."

"Are you serious, Dad?" Molly said.

"Absolutely."

"Can the Misfits use the control booth as our hangout?" Liam asked.

"What do you know about a control booth in there?" Lloyd asked.

"Oh, uh ... well ... nothing, really," Sarah added. "But you know, there probably is one."

"Hmmm. True. I guess you can as long as it's okay with your moms and you promise to do some work around the store."

"Are you kidding? That would be awesome," Connor said.

"Looks like the Mud Street Misfits have found a headquarters," David said and grinned.

"And a mascot." Sarah pointed down to where the puppy rooted around Steve Lewis' shoes.

**

The Misfits stood shoulder to shoulder, looking across the street at the Orpheum. The caution tape had been removed and someone, Sarah suspected it was Liam and Molly's dad, had scrubbed the decades of grime off the glass doors. It made the whole building shine and it looked eager to begin its new life.

"What a day," Liam said.

"A very cool day," Molly added.

"One of the best ever," Sarah agreed. "Thank you, guys."

"We make a great team," Connor said.

"I'm so glad you don't have to move to Chicago." Molly took Sarah's hand.

"Me, too. I'm so relieved that Mom-Heather convinced Mom-Rachel to stay." Sarah squeezed Molly's fingers.

"I can't wait to see what my dad does with the building," Liam said. "The control room will be perfect for the Misfits headquarters."

"Wouldn't it be awesome if he sold used records. You know, besides musical instruments?" Connor asked. "I could really help him with that."

"Uh, guys." David nudged Sarah's side and pointed.

"What?" It took her a minute to realize what she was seeing.

Framed in the entry way doors was a woman with gray frizzy hair. She held a slender cigarette in one hand and lifted the other to blow a kiss. When she did, a warm breeze ruffled Sarah's hair. She waved back and, slowly, Audrey faded from view.

"Please tell me you all saw that," Sarah said.

"If you mean the woman in the glass doors, then yes." Molly laughed.

"Did we just see a ghost?" Connor gaped.

Sarah giggled and clapped him on the back. "How's that for an adventure?"

"Very cool," he whispered, still staring at the door. "When can we do it again?"

"I always wanted to see a ghost," Molly said. "Maybe next time, a zombie."

They walked toward their bikes, but Sarah paused and glanced back over her shoulder at the beautiful old building that she'd helped save. It seemed to smile at her and she could feel its love and gratitude. "You're welcome," she whispered, then hurried after her friends.

As they pedaled around the corner toward Mud Street, Liam stopped next to the light pole at the entrance. A yellow flyer, held tenuously with tape, flapped in the breeze. He pulled it off, read it quickly, and turned to the others. "This is a notice about Camp Kachina. It says that it's going to be shut down after this summer. This is the last year."

"What? I love that camp," Molly said. "We're going to be Buffalos this year, right David?"

David snatched the flyer from Liam and studied it. Finally, he looked up at his friends. "Shutting down Camp Kachina? I don't think so. Not if the Mud Street Misfits have anything to say about it."

ABOUT THE AUTHORS

After long days working in an office, Brian spent many nights reading books and telling stories of adventures to his four children. Building off inspiration from his family, the stories became bigger and more animated and the request for stories became more frequent. Brian has always told his children to explore the world and chase their dreams. With encouragement and support from his family, Brian made the decision to follow one of his own dreams, writing down and sharing his stories with other Misfits!!

A Misfit herself, Beth's fascination with all things "woo-woo" goes back to her childhood where she spent many hours in fantasy worlds of her own creation. As an adult, knowing there was more to life than just what we see with our eyes, she began an exploration of these captivating other realms. A love of writing and the desire to share her knowledge sparked the creation of many short stories. Now, Beth is excited to share her love of the unknown with a new generation of readers and fellow Misfits